What really happened to the most notorious dog in town?

"Anyway," ZeeBee forges on. "That's why I haven't figured out who the murderer is yet. Because everybody on Centerlight is basically a suspect."

"Or nobody is," I remind her, releasing the spaniel with a pat on his haunches. "You know, if Barney died of natural causes. That makes a lot more sense than a phantom dog killer on the loose on a sleepy island like this."

She stares at me. "You're kidding, right? Centerlight—sleepy? This place is the gangster capital of North America."

ALSO BY GORDON KORMAN

NOTORIOUS

GORDON KORMAN

BALZER + BRAY
An Imprint of HarperCollinsPublishers

Balzer + Bray is an imprint of HarperCollins Publishers.

Library of Congress Cataloging-in-Publication Data

Names: Korman, Gordon, author.
Title: Notorious / Gordon Korman.
Description: First edition. | New York, NY : Balzer + Bray, an imprint of
  HarperCollinsPublishers, [2020] | Summary: Told in different voices, on
  Centerlight Island, halfway between the United States and Canada, middle-
  schoolers Keenan and ZeeBee team up to seek gold rumored to be hidden there by
  a famous gangster.
Identifiers: LCCN 2019010133 | ISBN 978-0-06-279887-9 (pbk.)
Subjects: | CYAC: Friendship—Fiction. | Middle schools—Fiction. |
  Schools—Fiction. | Buried treasure—Fiction. | Islands—Fiction.
Classification: LCC PZ7.K8369 Nq 2020 | DDC [Fic]—dc23 LC record available
  at https://lccn.loc.gov/2019010133

Typography by Erin Fitzsimmons
21 22 23 24   PC/BRR   10 9 8 7 6 5 4 3 2

First paperback edition, 2021

For Jesse and Tamara Toro

1

Keenan

You've probably seen the video—it's been viewed over eighteen million times.

A kitten has just slipped and fallen into a pond. All these geese are going nuts—flapping, honking, and making the poor little cat's panic fifty times worse than it already is. Suddenly, a big dog—maybe a chocolate Lab?—jumps into the water and paddles over, trying to grab the kitten by the scruff of the neck. It's

1

a matter of life and death. The kitten is struggling—about to go under.

"Grab him!" I'm yelling encouragement like a doofus. "You can do it!"

Just as the dog gets close, one of the geese flaps in his face, driving him back. But the Lab doesn't give up. The exhausted kitten drops below the surface. The dog lunges forward, sticking his snout underwater in a desperate attempt to—

The screen flickers once and goes dark.

"No-o-o!" I howl.

Desperately, I press the power button, and the dead battery icon appears on the screen. Ouch.

I'm not really worried about the cat, although it's hard not to get caught up in the heat of the moment. The title of the video was "Hero Dog Saves Drowning Kitten," so I'm pretty sure everything came out okay. The problem is my phone. It's at zero already and it's barely afternoon. Yesterday it lasted until almost two thirty. Now my only source of entertainment is the strap on the lawn chair that's cutting into my butt.

If I wasn't so tired, I'd move. But what would be the point? A different strap would cut into a different part of my body, and then I'd definitely be too tired to move again.

Dr. Sobel says I'll get my energy back as I continue to recover, but it's going to take a long time. That's how tuberculosis works. I don't even know where I picked it up. It could have been in any of the countries where my mom and my stepdad, Klaus, worked—China, because that's where we've lived for the past year. But it could also have been Montenegro, where we went on vacation, or even Lesotho, where we were before Shanghai. According to the doctor, the germs can live in your body for years before you get sick. But when you finally do, watch out. It feels like someone parked a locomotive on your chest. You can't stop coughing, which isn't fun because you ache all over. And lifting a paper clip takes all the energy you've got.

Forget staying in Shanghai, where Mom and Klaus teach at an international school. My dad made a huge stink that I had to come back to the States for my treatment. So here I am, shivering with a low-grade fever under a blanket in his backyard, staring at Canada.

That's right, I said Canada. Dad lives on Centerlight Island, Michigan, in the middle of the St. Clair River. In this area, the river is the dividing line between the United States and Canada. The border cuts right down the middle of the island in a zigzag. So I'm lying

3

here recovering in Michigan, but the cloud I'm staring up at—the one that looks like a giraffe with no legs—is actually over the province of Ontario. The Quayle sisters—these two old ladies three houses down in that direction—they're in Canada too.

If that seems complicated, downtown is even worse. The border goes right through it, dividing the post office building in half. One side sells American stamps and the other sells Canadian ones. If you fill up with gas and you want to get your car washed afterward, you have to cross an international line. Dad says the bowling alley is the only place on earth where you can throw a strike in another country.

There are no fences, no checkpoints, no guys asking to look at your passport. I've been all over the world, and I'm positive that there's no place quite like this. People cross the border maybe ten times a day just living their normal lives. If GameStop is in Canada, that's where you go to buy an extra controller for your Xbox. There are barely enough customers around here to fill one town, let alone two.

No offense, but coming from the big cities I've lived in, Centerlight is pretty one-horse. Not that I've got the strength to do anything fun even if there was something fun to do. There isn't. That chair strap digging into my butt? It's the highlight of my day. In Shanghai, I'd visit friends on a train that levitates above the track thanks to a system of futuristic magnets. The closest we have to that here is refrigerator magnets.

My job? Lie here and get better . . . slowly. Agonizingly slowly. I can't even watch TV, because Dr. Sobel wants me outside in the fresh air. I stream videos and play games on my phone until the battery dies. I've got the summer reading list for my grade, but I can't find the motivation to pick up a book. School starts in three weeks, and there's no way Dad and Dr. Sobel will give me a clean bill of health to fly back by then. And it's not like any of my teachers from seven thousand miles away are going to randomly show up here of all places and catch me goofing off.

I know that sounds lazy. I *am* lazy. It's not my fault. Tuberculosis makes you lazy. Besides, even if I wanted to do something, I probably wouldn't be allowed to—I might cough on someone. Although I'm coughing a lot less than before. That's a good sign. If I can start school in September, and it doesn't kill me, and every kid on the island doesn't immediately come down with TB, then maybe Dad will give the okay for me to go back to my life in Shanghai. That's what I'm hoping for, anyway.

I guess the word I'm working toward is *boring*. I'm *so* bored. I didn't know it was possible to be this bored and still be alive. I've been staring at the same bushes for so long that I swear they're staring back at me.

And then the bushes *blink*.

At first, I'm not even surprised. I could be dreaming. Sometimes I doze off just because there's nothing worth staying awake for. But no—this is real. There's a pair of eyes on the other side of the hedge, staring at me.

I sit bolt upright. It's kind of impressive. I haven't moved that fast since I got TB. It gives me a bit of a head rush.

"Who's there?" I croak.

"Oh, hi!" comes a voice. There's a rustling and this girl squeezes right through the bushes, her hands protecting her face from the scratching branches. She's about my age, blond, skinny, with a heart-shaped face and huge inquiring blue eyes. Her T-shirt features a red maple leaf curled into a fist, with the message: *Yeah, I'm Canadian. You want to make something out of it?*

A moment later, the bushes stir again, and a dog passes through, scrabbling on its belly. A cocker spaniel—blond as the girl—hurries to keep pace with her.

I perk up immediately at the sight of the dog. Then I remember.

"Don't come too close!" I order the girl. "I could still be contagious."

She halts her progress, but doesn't look worried. "You know, if you're sick, you should really stay inside."

"It's tuberculosis," I tell her. "I'm supposed to get as much fresh air as I can."

"Yeah, right," she says sarcastically. "And I've got bubonic plague, so we should get along fine."

"I'm serious! I have tuberculosis. I got it in Asia. Or Africa. Maybe Europe."

She grins. "Why not Australia?"

"I've never lived in Australia. I've lived in all those other places. My mom teaches at international schools." I see her glancing toward the house, a frown on her face. "This is my *dad's* house. He works at GM in Detroit."

She rolls her eyes. "Americans are so lucky. You've got a bridge to the mainland."

I'm mystified. "The bridge has a no-Canadians rule?"

"Of course not. But it goes to the wrong side. If you

7

want to get to Canada, you have to take the ferry. Let me tell you, that's not exactly fun when I'm crossing the river to school in January with snow blowing into my face."

"You don't go to the school right here in town?" I ask.

She shakes her head. "That's a *Michigan* school. I have to graduate in *Ontario*, and we don't have a school on Centerlight. Most of the Canadians on the island are retirees—not a lot of kids. The nearest school for us is in Corunna, and that means a boat ride." She stretches out her hand. "I'm ZeeBee."

I pull away from it. "I told you, I might be contagious." I add, "I'm Keenan."

"My real name is Zarabeth," she explains, "but who wants to be that? My parents got it from this classic *Star Trek* episode. They're a couple of old nerds."

ZeeBee doesn't interest me all that much. But her dog is another story. The spaniel—whose eyes are even bigger than ZeeBee's—is doing everything but jump through hoops trying to get her to notice him.

"Who's your friend?"

She frowns. "Friend?"

I point. "The one licking your ankle."

"Oh, this is just Barney Two," she replies, shaking

the spaniel off her leg. The little dog lands flat on his face on the grass, then bounces right up, eager to spar another round. He's a total ball of energy. Yet at the same time, he's really well behaved. Despite his high spirits, he never barks beyond the occasional yip. His gaze rarely strays from his owner, seeking attention.

"Barney Two?" I echo. "Is there a Barney One?"

"There used to be. He was murdered."

I choke, which sets off a little of the TB cough. "Murdered?"

Her face is grim. "Not everybody thinks so. He was fifteen—that's pretty old for a big dog. But it was murder. I'd bet my life on it."

"How can you be so sure?"

"Everybody hated Barney," she explains. "Canadians. Americans. It was the only thing everyone agreed on around here. It didn't matter what side of the border you were from."

She looks so sad that I'm moved to say, "Come on, it can't be that bad."

"You never met Barney," she insists mournfully. "We couldn't keep him tied up. He always got away. We had a six-foot fence. He jumped it. And once he was loose, he roamed all over the island, digging, barking, and pooping wherever he pleased. He growled at people and even bit them if they didn't back off. He broke into the supermarket and ransacked the food. He howled so loud you could hear it on the mainland in both countries. He was part mastiff, so he was gigantic. He was part rottweiler, so nothing scared him. And he was part Newfoundland, so if the cops came after him, he just jumped in the river and paddled away with his webbed feet. He hated other dogs—he didn't have a single friend. Except me. I didn't hate Barney. I loved him. Someone had to."

For the first time, I almost relate to her. I love dogs. We used to have one—Fluffy. But when my folks split, Dad didn't want to keep her, and Mom and I were heading overseas for her first international school gig. I don't remember much about Fluffy, except that she would follow me around all day and curl up with me at night. I was only five. I hope Dad wasn't lying when he told me she went to a good family with lots of kids to play with. How I hated those kids. I used to lie in bed in Mumbai and picture a bunch of random strangers having fun with *my* dog.

At least Dad didn't say Fluffy went to live on a farm. That would have been a dead giveaway.

"We move to a different country practically every year," I volunteer. "My mom and Klaus don't think it would be practical to get a pet."

ZeeBee nods sympathetically. "How clueless are parents? They never understand. My folks thought getting Barney Two would make me feel better." She scowls at the spaniel at her feet. "Like this jumped-up chipmunk could ever replace my Barney."

It sounds to me as if nothing less than a rampaging T. Rex could replace her Barney. Aloud, I say, "He's a cute little guy. And he's definitely nuts about you."

"Exactly." She's triumphant. "Barney would never grovel at somebody's sneakers. Knock over their garden shed, maybe. Or push their snowmobile into the river."

I reach down to pat Barney Two, but he shies away. He only has eyes for ZeeBee—not that she gives him a nanosecond's notice. Poor little guy. I pat my leg a couple of times and he finally trots over. I scratch his neck and roll him onto his back and rub his belly. He squirms with pleasure. Even so, every few seconds, he gazes up at his owner to make sure she's okay with it. She never even glances his way.

"It's safe," I tell ZeeBee. "TB never travels from humans to animals."

She has no idea what I'm talking about. "Anyway," she forges on. "That's why I haven't figured out who the murderer is yet. Because everybody on Centerlight is basically a suspect."

"Or nobody is," I remind her, releasing the spaniel with a pat on his silky haunches. "You know, if Barney died of natural causes. That makes a lot more sense than a phantom dog killer on the loose on a sleepy island like this."

She stares at me. "You're kidding, right? Centerlight—sleepy? This place is the gangster capital of North America."

I actually sit up and look around. I have no idea what I expect to see. Criminals standing six deep around my dad's yard?

"Well, not so much *now*," she explains. "But back in the twenties and thirties this was the number-one smuggling route for rumrunners sneaking liquor from Canada into the U.S. During Prohibition, half the houses on the Canadian side used to be owned by mobsters who were staying out of the reach of the FBI. Guess who lived in my house—Tommy-Gun Ferguson! Can you believe that?"

"Who's Tommy-Gun Ferguson?"

She shakes her head in amazement. "You really aren't from around here. Thomas 'Tommy-Gun' Ferguson was Al Capone's main connection in the liquor business. They made millions together—and that was back in the days when a candy bar cost a nickel and you could go to a movie for twenty-five cents. The feds got him eventually and he died in prison. But no one ever found what he did with his money."

I cock an eyebrow at her. "Are you saying it's hidden in your house?"

"Nah, Barney would have sniffed it out. He might have been part bloodhound too. But a lot of people say Tommy-Gun Ferguson converted his fortune into gold and stashed it somewhere on the island. And if that's true, whoever finds it is going to be filthy rich."

It's around this point that a little switch flips in my head. The dog murder I can sort of believe since Barney One sounds like a total winner. I can even swallow some of the gangster stuff, because Prohibition was a real thing back in the twenties and thirties. But I call baloney at Tommy-Gun Ferguson and his secret stash of gold. I may be a newbie here, and I admit I was pretty sick when my father brought me home to start treatment. But this isn't my first trip to Centerlight. Dad moved here three years after the divorce, and I visit at least once a summer. If the whole island was swarming with shovel-wielding treasure hunters searching for buried treasure, I'm pretty sure I would have noticed.

"It isn't just Tommy-Gun Ferguson," ZeeBee goes on. "This place used to be crawling with gangsters. Al Capone himself brought his family here every summer. He said it was vacation, but a lot of 'unlucky' people always happened to get killed when he was around. Eliot Ness came here too—the famous lawman. Where else could you keep an eye on gangsters from New York, Atlantic City, Miami, Chicago, and Detroit all in one place? They even ate at the same restaurant—Fanelli's on Main Street. It's a Taco Bell now, but out by the drive-thru there's still the original wall with seven bullet holes from a machine gun. There's a stain on the pavement. They say it's salsa, but don't you believe it. Salsa washes away. Blood never does. I'll take you there."

"Can't," I put in quickly. "I'm not supposed to leave the yard." Dr. Sobel didn't actually warn me not to run around the island looking at gangster blood, but I'm sure he would have if he'd thought of it.

"I mean when your trichinosis goes away," she says.

"Tuberculosis!" I snap back.

"Whatever. I can also show you the lighthouse—the

gangsters used to shoot out the beacon so the cops couldn't see when a shipment was coming ashore. I think they tried to burn it down a couple of times too. It's not in the greatest shape. And you've got to see Snitch's Rock—that was Tommy-Gun's favorite place to get rid of witnesses before they could testify against him."

She goes on and on. Who got shot here; who got arrested there; which truckload of booze went out of control and crashed into Our Lady of Temperance. By this time I'm not doubting what she tells me anymore; I'm 100 percent convinced that ZeeBee—Zarabeth, whatever—is a certified nutcase. Barney Two trots in slow circles around her, wagging his cropped tail. The faster her mouth goes, the faster the tail wags, and that's pretty fast. I feel sorry for him. He's such a cute little guy. Fluffy was like that. Not physically—I think Fluffy was part schnauzer. I mean that *lovable*.

A distant foghorn sounds, a long mournful honk.

"Well, that's me," she says suddenly.

I'm bug-eyed. "That's *you*?"

"My dad. He's a Canadian border officer. When he heads in on the boat, he always gives us a toot to let us know he's on the way. Don't worry, I'll be back tomorrow."

My first instinct is to say, *I won't be here tomorrow.* But who am I kidding? Where else am I going to be? And anyway, ZeeBee is already gone, scrunched through the bushes, her unappreciated dog at her heels.

2

Zarabeth

Nobody appreciates a good lighthouse anymore.

The one on Centrelight is 160 years old. That dates back to the days when boats really needed a lighthouse to keep from crashing into rocks and things because they didn't have running lights of their own. It's a national treasure—two national treasures really, since it's built right on the border that cuts through the island. The problem is it needs six million dollars' worth of repairs. And for that much money,

Canada wants it to be an American national treasure, and the Americans want to give it to us. Meanwhile, somebody has to run it, so the two countries switch days. The U.S. takes Monday, Wednesday, Friday, and Canada gets Tuesday, Thursday, Saturday. (We alternate Sundays.)

Luckily, nobody has to sit up there like in the old days. The system is automated now, so all it needs is someone to be on call in case of breakdown. The Americans outsource the job to the company that maintains the computer system. But Canada makes the border service run it, which means my dad has to take his turn like the other officers. We get a phone call when the light burns out at four o'clock in the morning. That's actually happened more than once. It's hard to get back to sleep after a lighthouse call.

It's too bad that the future of an amazing old lighthouse is in jeopardy just because of money. But that's the way of the world, I guess. It costs a lot to run a whole country, and neither one wants to spend a fortune on a little island in the middle of nowhere. That goes double for Canada, because, even though we have half the land of Centrelight, there are only twelve hundred of us Canadians living here, compared with over five thousand Americans. Don't I know that! When I get on the ferry to go to school on the mainland, there are only ten other kids with me—four high schoolers and six little kids. Not a single one is even close to my age. I used to at least have my brother, Wayne, to talk to, but he's away at university now in Toronto.

Standing on the dock, waiting for the boat, you can see the top of Centrelight Middle School—actually, Centerlight Middle School, that's how the Americans spell it. Four hundred kids go there. Although the Americans have more than 80 percent of the people, they have more like 99 percent of the kids. Centrelight is a great place for the Michigan families because you can have island living, but thanks to the bridge, you can be on the mainland and heading for Detroit or some other city in just a few minutes.

It kind of stinks because it's hard to make friends with kids you don't go to school with. And the kids I *do* go to school with live on the mainland, which might as well be on the moon. I used to have Barney, and that was more than enough. Just wheedling him out of trouble was a full-time job. But in the end, I blew it, didn't I?

I push the thought out of my mind. It makes me too sad.

Barney Two isn't much of a replacement. He wouldn't

get into trouble if you put ten thousand volts through him. No personality at all.

That's why I was lucky to find Keenan. He's a captive audience since he's stuck in that lawn chair all day while his lungs get better. Perfect timing too, because during summer, nobody cares who goes to what school. But there's a nice balance to our friendship. I give him pointers on Centrelight life, and he looks out for me by not coughing in my direction and giving me tuberculosis.

The third day I go over there, I bring along a few welcome gifts:

A postcard of our historic lighthouse. It's a great picture, taken a long time ago, before the pieces started falling off. Also, the Canadian flag is flying, which only happens half the time.

A tourist map of the island, showing the Canada-U.S. border, which looks like a piece of modern art the way it squiggles around.

A Centrelight History souvenir keychain, with a double-headed portrait: Al Capone on one side and Eliot Ness on the other.

One order of poutine, the most Canadian food ever.

He looks at the takeout container like it's filled with live scorpions.

"It's French fries with gravy and cheese curds," I supply. "If you're going to live in Canada, you might as well get used to it."

"I *don't* live in Canada," he reminds me.

"Around here, if you worry too much about the border, you'll go crazy. Pass gas anywhere in Centrelight, they smell it in two different countries." I indicate the poutine. "Try it. Trust me, it's a lot less gross than it looks."

"Your little friend thinks so too." Keenan nods in the direction of Barney Two, who peers longingly up at the container, panting quietly.

I back him off with my sneaker. "Forget it, buster." I can't help thinking of Original Barney, who would have skipped the begging part and wolfed down the food, the container, and probably most of my arm below the elbow. This purebred impostor is an insult to the proud Barney name.

Keenan examines the fries. "How come there are fingerprints in the gravy?"

"I love poutine," I tell him. "Hey, I'm not the one with the tuberculosis," I add when he scowls at me. "Once *you* take a bite, the whole batch is contaminated."

"Maybe not," he argues in his own defense. "My doctor says I'm probably not contagious anymore."

"So let's blow this popsicle stand!" I exclaim. "I can't wait to show you around the island."

"Not yet," he puts in quickly. "I'm getting better, but I still have to take it easy."

Bummer. As much as I like Keenan, being stuck in this one little backyard is getting on my nerves. Barney and I had that in common. We didn't appreciate being fenced in. Wimpy Barney Two couldn't care less.

Keenan reaches under the lawn chair and pulls out a tennis ball. He holds it under Barney Two's wet nose for a few seconds and then launches it across the yard.

Barney Two doesn't move a muscle.

"C'mon, boy—fetch!" Keenan encourages.

"He might actually be too stupid to understand," I offer.

"And Barney One had a PhD in fetching, I suppose," Keenan says sarcastically.

"Barney wouldn't have chased it either," I admit.

"He had better things to do with his time."

Keenan seems annoyed. "Barney Two is *not* stupid. In fact, he's the opposite. He isn't fetching because he's waiting for permission."

I'm amazed. "What does he expect—an engraved invitation?"

"I mean permission from *you*."

"Why should he care what I say?" Keenan might have a point, though. Barney Two is looking up at me as if awaiting some kind of signal. "Fine," I tell the dog. "You can go."

Barney Two takes off across the lawn like he's been shot from a cannon. His gait is so fast and so light that his paws barely disturb the individual blades of grass. I can't help but compare it to any one of Barney's many rampages.

On the fly, he scoops up the ball, turns on a dime, and races back to hold it out to me.

"What am I supposed to do with it?" I ask him.

Keenan reaches over to take back the ball, but Barney Two bites down on it with his teeth. Pretty soon there's a mini tug-of-war going on, with Keenan pulling and twisting, and the dog clamped on alligator-style. The craziest part is that Keenan is smiling and laughing like he's never had so much fun. Honestly, it's the happiest I've ever seen him. (*Ever* meaning the past three days.)

"Okay, enough. Stop," I say.

Barney Two drops the tennis ball like a hot potato.

"I brought something else," I tell Keenan. "You can't keep this because it's probably worth a lot of money." I reach into my pocket and take out an ancient bullet shell casing, the brass tarnished. "We found this on our property when we dug the hole for Barney's grave. It's probably from Tommy-Gun Ferguson—maybe even from the famous gun that gave him his name."

"Or some random guy shooting at tin cans," he comments.

I shake my head vigorously. "This is Centrelight. You find a bullet here, and it was either shot *by* a gangster, *at* a gangster, or *through* a gangster."

He laughs. "Prohibition was like ninety years ago."

I step closer (I hope he really isn't contagious any-more) and drop my voice. "Listen, just because the rumrunners are gone doesn't mean there are no more gangsters on Centrelight. The laws may be different, but we're still right on the border, and that's a valuable location for illegal activities."

"What illegal activities?" he asks, licking the gravy off a French fry. "Smuggling poutine? Maybe it just oozes across the line."

"Things happen here," I confide in a hushed tone. "People meet and have secret conversations in the middle of the night. Strangers suddenly appear and then you never see them again. Car alarms go off for no reason. There are footprints that can't be explained and voices that are almost, but not quite, heard. Someone's watching our house, Keenan. I don't make mistakes about things like that. My father is a law enforcement professional, so I've got it in my DNA."

He frowns. "Then shouldn't you be telling him, and not me?"

"He's not a cop; he's a border officer," I explain. "He works on the river. You can't enforce the border on the island. It's just not possible. His only responsibility on Centrelight is lighthouse duty."

"Yeah, but if somebody's watching your *house* . . ."

I feel my cheeks flame. "My father doesn't believe me about that. He says I'm being too dramatic."

I can tell by the look on Keenan's face that he agrees with Dad. It kind of annoys me. How long has he been here? Five minutes? I'm the one who knows everything there is to know about Centrelight.

"Eat your poutine," I tell him. "It's no good when it's cold."

3

Keenan

The call comes in at the worst possible moment. It's almost lunchtime Wednesday, and I've been playing Igloo Tycoon all morning. I'm only three blocks away from completing the Alaskan Edifice, which would be a personal best for me. But my phone is down to 4 percent, so if I take the call and the battery dies on me, I'll lose all my progress.

It's an easy decision—until Dad's work number

appears across the frozen tundra. With a sigh, I hit Accept.

"Hey, kid. How's it going?" he greets me. "Just got the test results from Dr. Sobel. Good news—you're golden. You've still got to take your meds, but you've got the green light to leave the house."

"Really?" I'm psyched. "How long before I can go back to Shanghai?"

"Not so fast," he cautions. "You're not getting rid of your old man so easily."

"That's not what I meant, Dad," I say, instantly contrite.

"It's still going to take a while for your immune system to rebuild itself. The last thing you need is sixteen hours on a plane, breathing people's recycled germs." He adds, "We talked about this, remember?"

"I remember." The one topic that never came up in that conversation was the time frame. I get that I'm stuck here, but till when? It's starting to sink in that I never asked because I didn't want to hear the answer.

"It's just that I really don't know anybody on Centerlight." Not technically true. I know ZeeBee. I'll bet there's nobody quite like her, even in Shanghai, with its twenty-four million residents.

"All that's going to change now that you can get out," Dad reasons. "You'll meet people—especially when school starts in a couple of weeks."

"Right." I guess I sound pretty dejected. I was hoping to get back to Mom and Klaus and my friends pretty soon after my clean bill of health. Now Dad's implying that not only am I here until school starts, but that I'll be staying awhile. Bummer. When you're on the international school circuit, your classmates are from all over the world—kids of ambassadors and princes, professors and tycoons. You live in exciting cities, where you hear more different languages before lunch than you'll hear in a century in Centerlight. Face it, a remote little island is just plain dull, no matter who shot who during Prohibition ninety years ago.

"You'll want to get your strength back by the time school rolls around," Dad goes on. "So I signed you up for some training sessions at Island Fitness. It's on the American side, next door to Taco Bell. Ask for Bryce. On the phone, he sounded like a really good guy. He works out a lot of kids. He's a Chicago boy, just like your old man. Same neighborhood too—west side. Of course, he's a little younger than me."

"Of course," I echo cautiously.

He sweetens the pot. "And guess what—Bryce used to be an amateur MMA fighter. How cool is that? You're still into jujitsu, right?"

"Tae kwon do," I correct him. "I picked it up when we lived in Korea, but I've studied it other places too."

"See? You two have something in common already," Dad concludes. "You've got a two-fifteen appointment. Enjoy." A command, not a suggestion.

So help me, it actually does sound pretty good. To go somewhere—anywhere—that isn't either the house or the yard. I'll go for a training session. I'll go for being-hit-on-the-head lessons if it'll pull me off the lawn chair and set me on the road to getting my life back.

Stepping out the front door of the house is a weird experience. I've been on Centerlight for more than a month, but except for past visits and a few car rides to the doctor, I haven't really seen much of it. As I walk along St. Clair Avenue toward downtown, I'm amazed at how quickly I'm out of breath. That's what you get for weeks of lying on your butt. I'm about to take a major L at Island Fitness. I hope this guy Bryce isn't expecting a sparring partner, because what he's getting is more like a paperweight.

Downtown is less than half a mile away, but I'm in

no shape to hoof it. I find a bench and sink down on it gratefully. I haven't been there long when a small jitney bus pulls up to the curb. It's covered in overlapping American and Canadian flags, with a sign reading: SEE HISTORIC CENTERLIGHT. The driver opens the door and looks at me expectantly.

"Going downtown?" I ask.

"Hop on."

To my surprise, the jitney is full of *tourists*—not a crowd, but at least seven or eight. I look at this island as a place you go as a last resort to recover from a serious illness, but there are people who come here on vacation—on *purpose*.

I take a seat next to an older lady who is poring over a "gangster map" of the island. I peer over her shoulder at the different destinations—Al Capone's waterfront home, Bugs Moran's cottage, Meyer Lansky's summer rental, and the rooming house where Eliot Ness and his famous Untouchables stayed during trips to Centerlight are marked in boldfaced type. Lesser figures and mob lieutenants appear in smaller print. I blink. Tommy-Gun Ferguson is on there too. I half believed ZeeBee made him up. But there's his house—a wood-frame Victorian with a cupola and a wraparound balcony. Which means that must be *ZeeBee*'s house. I pictured it as being kind of far because it's in another country. But it's only a few blocks away from Dad's, even if it's on the other side of the border. No wonder she and Barney Two show up in our yard every single day. It's just a short walk from home.

For me, it's an eye-opener. ZeeBee seems kind of crazy, but all this gangster stuff turns out to be real—real enough to bring vacationers to Centerlight to tour the island, following maps of gangster homes!

When we reach Island Fitness, the bus empties out. I'm the only one going to the gym; everybody else wants to see Lucky Luciano's bocce court, which is in the back of a dark tavern called Volstead's.

Bryce Bergstrom, my trainer, turns out to be a twenty-two-year-old tower of muscle with a blond brush cut and tattoos along both arms. Yeah, I'll say he's a little younger than Dad. And there are a few other differences—like the fact that he's a tank.

He looks me up and down. "So you're the martial artist."

"More like I'm the kid who can't string together three decent breaths," I confess.

"I don't do excuses," he tells me seriously.

The gym is about equally split between weights on one side and cardio equipment on the other. Bryce sets me up on a leg press machine, and at first I'm amazed how easy it is to move the stack.

Bryce counts in a strident voice that reminds me of a marine drill sergeant. "One! . . . Two! . . . Three! . . ."

But somewhere between four and five, something happens. I feel like my lungs are being squeezed in a giant vise grip, and I'm sucking for air that just won't come.

"Sorry," I pant, rolling out of the seat and collapsing into a squat on the padded floor. "I had tuberculosis. I know, excuses—"

"Take your time," he insists, somehow managing to sound impatient about it. Or maybe I'm putting that on myself. Something about this bodybuilder makes me want to impress him.

Bryce runs me through a routine of free weights, machines, and abdominal exercises, and each time it's the same. I start out great—strong, even. But a few reps in, I run out of breath. The weights slam down against the stacks and I'm left gasping.

"Good," says Bryce.

"Good?" I wheeze with what little wind I have left. "I can't do anything. What's so good about that? I have no strength left!"

He shakes his head. "You have plenty of strength.

What you need is *stamina*."

"Now who's making excuses?"

He favors me with a crooked grin. "It doesn't count when I do it."

It's the first time I see Bryce smile. He's like a whole different person when it happens. His face becomes softer, less angular.

"Now we've got something to shoot for," he goes on, escorting me to a treadmill. "Cardio."

It's a disaster. I can't jog, and when Bryce lowers my speed to a walk, I run out of steam after thirty seconds.

At first, even he seems frustrated. Then he hands me a pair of boxing gloves.

I stare at him. "Boxing?"

He shakes his head. "*Kick*boxing. Let's go. Shoes off."

"There's no way I'm going to be able to do this."

"Excuses," he repeats, cutting me off.

He slips his hands into pads, and I offer a couple of weak pokes with my gloves.

"Come *on*!" he barks.

It's when I try my first kick that it all starts to gel. I've been taking tae kwon do since I was eight, and the moves come back as if my body has its own memory. I punch and kick at the padding, my confidence growing.

Bryce doesn't say anything, but his expression is one of deep approval. All at once, I'm overcome by the urge to blow his mind. The next time he raises a pad to shoulder level, I resolve to hit it with a flying kick.

I know I'm not going to make it even before I let the kick go. My foot hits nothing but thin air and the rest of me hits the mat like a ton of bricks. I'm so dazed that Bryce makes me sit there for a while before hauling me upright again.

"Sorry," I mumble. "I used to be able to nail that."

"And you'll nail it again," he promises. "You did great!"

"Yeah," I muse, toying with the idea of being a little impressed with myself. "Especially if you consider I had tuber—"

Bryce raises a palm the size of a dinner plate. "No 'if you consider.' No excuses. You showed up today. That's a good thing. End of story."

"I almost showed up in the emergency room," I say ruefully.

He shakes his head. "Believe in yourself, Keenan."

Still, he walks me to the door—which implies that

he doesn't trust me to make it outside without falling flat on my face.

I notice that a jagged red scar bisects the tattoo on the arm he uses to steady me.

"Wow," I comment. "Where'd you get that?"

He shrugs. "In the Octagon."

"That's right—you did MMA!" I just tried to cold-cock a real Ultimate Fighter. I'm part proud, part horrified.

"*Amateur* MMA," he amends.

"We don't do excuses here," I remind him.

"Wise guy. Your dad should have warned me about you." He indicates the scar. "It was a long time ago. A heavyweight who didn't believe in manicures. Fingernails and stitches go together in MMA."

Yikes. Hospitals. Doctors. I can relate.

A loud blast from a horn nearly launches me out of my skin. ZeeBee sits in the passenger seat of a jeep marked *Canada Border Services*. Barney Two is on the dashboard, batting at the air freshener with one paw. Seeing that little guy always makes me smile.

"I thought you weren't allowed out of the backyard," ZeeBee calls, a little accusingly.

I grin. "First day of freedom. My dad signed me up

for the gym to get my strength back. This is Bryce, my trainer. Bryce, ZeeBee."

"I've seen you around," Bryce tells her.

"Everybody sees everybody around on Centerlight," ZeeBee explains for my benefit.

"I'm starting to get the picture," I say.

The spaniel darts out and interposes himself protectively between Bryce and the jeep.

"That's okay, Barney Two," I soothe. "Bryce is a friend."

"Barney *Two*?" the trainer queries.

"Their old dog was Barney One," I explain. I almost add *He was murdered*, but stop myself at the last second. When you spend too much time with ZeeBee, you almost forget how nuts the things she says might sound to somebody else.

"He was just Barney," ZeeBee calls. "There can never be another one."

A middle-aged man in a short-sleeved blue uniform steps out of the pharmacy and gets in behind the wheel.

"Dad, this is that kid I was telling you about—Keenan."

He looks me up and down. "American, eh? Well, nobody's perfect."

"Stop it, Dad," ZeeBee pleads from the jeep. To me, she adds, "He's *joking*."

I peer past ZeeBee's father to the next block over, where the post office sits. Sure enough, an American flag flies from the near entrance, and the red maple leaf of Canada flutters over the far door. That would mean that the white line painted along the main road that disappears into the building must be the famous border. I feel an odd urge to dash across it just to see if ZeeBee's father tackles me. Then again, in my current state, I couldn't dash if you put a booster rocket in my pants—that's why Bryce had to practically carry me out of the gym.

Remembering Bryce, I say, "Officer Tice, this is my trainer—" and that's when I notice I'm introducing thin air. "Oh, sorry. I guess he has another client or something."

"Can we give Keenan a ride home?" ZeeBee asks her father. "This is his first day out and he's probably tired."

The Canadian border officer nods. "Hop in. I hope you don't mind a little detour. I've got to swing by the lighthouse and check the computer system."

ZeeBee frowns. "The Americans are in charge on Wednesday."

I hope they don't expect me to do anything about it. Just because I'm American doesn't mean I know how to fix a lighthouse.

Officer Tice starts up the jeep and pulls away from the curb. "I know it's their day. But the Geek Squad blew a tire on the bridge, so that leaves me."

"You're not a computer expert," ZeeBee points out.

Her father shrugs. "If I can get my head around the rules of curling, I can figure this out too."

So we drive away from town and into the woods. For the last half mile or so, it's a dirt road. Barney Two slides off the dashboard and ZeeBee doesn't even seem to notice him landing in a heap on the floor of the jeep.

"You'll like the lighthouse," she tells me, oblivious to her dog's scrambling at her feet. "Except for the computer that runs it, it's no different than it was back in the 1860s."

"The bathroom's only been there since the 1980s," Officer Tice points out. "You've got Canada to thank for that."

"That was . . . nice of you," I volunteer because he seems to expect some comment.

"Nice my foot. They put the latrine on the American

side. That was before my time, obviously."

"Obviously," I gulp, hoping he's kidding.

I've only seen the lighthouse from a distance. It's kind of impressive—seven or eight stories tall and cobbled together with fieldstone. I know it's pretty old, but it *looks* older than the big bang. The closer you get, the more you can see how it's crumbling. There are a lot of gaps in the mortar holding the stones in place—and a lot of pieces lying on the ground at the foot of the tower.

"American flag," I note, seeing the Stars and Stripes fluttering above the beacon.

ZeeBee nods. "Until morning. Then we switch."

Officer Tice steps out of the jeep and beckons. "Come have a look. We're pretty proud of this old place."

I don't know what I expect the inside of a lighthouse to look like. This is basically a big stone tube, cool in spite of the heat of the day, with an earthy smell, like plant soil. There's the bathroom opposite the door, but otherwise the space is completely bare except for a wrought-iron spiral staircase rising in the center.

Officer Tice starts up, his footsteps gonging in the still air. ZeeBee follows, and of course Barney Two follows her. I'm right behind them—and I haven't gone very far before I realize what a bad idea this is. It's my first day off the lawn chair and the last thing I need is to go up and around, up and around to infinity. By the time I get to the top of the stairs, I'm almost too dizzy to think about what I'm seeing.

"This is the watch room," ZeeBee's dad explains. "Back in the day, this place was full of gears and pulleys and levers. Now all we need is that." He indicates a laptop computer sitting on a wooden table. He shakes the mouse. "Frozen again. Wouldn't you know it?" He pulls out the power cord, plugs it in again, and touches a button. The computer boots back to life.

He checks a few settings and nods. "All fixed. No Geek Squad necessary."

ZeeBee grabs my arm. "Let's check out the light!"

Like I'm not woozy enough, she drags me up a wooden ladder to the top level. It's all glass—ancient panes, most of them cracked. The beacon is bigger than I am—a giant spotlight surrounded by mirrors. If it was night and the beacon was lit, it would be projecting our shadows all along the St. Clair River.

"There it is—the whole island." She gestures at the panorama laid out before us.

She's expecting me to be impressed, and it's kind of nice, I guess. But when you've seen the pyramids and the Taj Mahal, it's hard to get all worked up over a slab of rocks and dirt. The U.S. on one side of the river, Canada on the other. And in the middle, good old Centerlight—a little bit of both, but also sort of neither.

Going down is even harder than going up—especially with Barney Two, who always seems to be wherever I'm trying to plant my foot.

Back on solid ground, Officer Tice regards me critically. "Better get you home, Keenan. You're a little green around the gills."

We pile into the jeep. ZeeBee shuts the passenger door, leaving Barney Two yelping plaintively on the cobblestones.

I open my door and pat the seat next to me. "Come on, Barney."

The spaniel leaps inside, but avoids my hand, squeezing to the front to be near ZeeBee.

She sounds annoyed. "He's *not* Barney. He isn't even close to Barney—and he's never going to be."

"Zarabeth," her father says reprovingly.

As we jounce along the dirt road, we pass the

black-and-white car from the Geek Squad driving gingerly toward the lighthouse.

"Aren't you going to tell them?" I ask ZeeBee's dad. "You know, that it's fixed already?"

The Canadian border officer doesn't answer. But I can see his smile in the rearview mirror.

4

Zarabeth

According to the internet, tuberculosis is an infectious disease of the lungs, which causes fever, night sweats, weight loss, and mostly "cough with blood-containing sputum." I also found out that, in the old days, about half the people who got it died. I'm not super clear on when that was, but I assume that it means back before they had antibiotics to knock out the bacteria that cause TB. Keenan is still on antibiotics, despite the fact that he's better now and doesn't have to lie around his dad's backyard anymore. I also looked up *sputum*, but out of respect to Keenan, I'm not going to talk about it, even though it's a pretty cool word. Sometimes, when nobody's around except Barney Two, I say it out loud and think about the sound and not the meaning. It's actually kind of majestic, like some mythological creature—Sputum the Enchanted Dragon, who flies over the kingdom propelled by mighty wings. In reality, the only creatures that fly over Centrelight are the seagulls, and they're almost as gross as what sputum really is. (And what they drop everywhere is even worse.)

So Keenan wasn't just lying around to be lazy, and he didn't make up the part about being confined to the backyard because he was trying to avoid me. Not that he *could* avoid me even if he wanted to. I'm kind of unavoidable. I know the island like the back of my hand, and besides, I'm a border officer's daughter, so tracking people down comes naturally to me. Plus, just because Keenan's TB is cured doesn't mean he's 100 percent okay. He looked pretty pale after we climbed to the top of the lighthouse that day. So he'd never shake me, since I have the advantage in speed, stamina, and mastery of the terrain.

I know that sounds kind of military (and also a little

bit stalkerish). But nothing could be further from the truth. Poor Keenan is stuck here half a world away from his regular life in China. The fact that I'm a Centrelight expert makes me the perfect person to show him around. He's *lucky* I found him lying there, all alone in his dad's backyard, bored out of his mind, watching the grass grow. Now he won't be bored anymore.

My brother Wayne's old bike is big for me, but it looks exactly Keenan-size. It's a little tricky riding it— even lowering the seat, I can barely reach the pedals. I can't go very fast, which suits Barney Two just fine. He can't run very fast on those dumb stubby legs of his. My Barney ran like a gazelle—or at least a gazelle having a very bad hair day.

At Keenan's house, my dismount is a little undignified. Without any momentum to help me keep my balance, as soon as I stop, I keel over into the bushes.

So I'm scratched up and covered in leaves when I ring the doorbell. Keenan's face lights up at the sight of me.

"Hey, Barney Two! How's it going, boy?"

Figures. He's talking to the dog.

"In case you haven't noticed, I'm *injured*," I say in annoyance. "Tuberculosis isn't the only bad thing that

45

can happen to a person, you know."

He notices Wayne's bike and puts two and two together. "That's too big for you."

"No duh," I tell him. "But not too big for *you*. Here, try it out."

He gets on and rides up and down the driveway. Carefully—like he does everything. Maybe it's the TB, or maybe it's the kind of kid he is.

"Perfect fit," he pronounces. "But I don't want to buy a bike. I'll be going home soon."

I feel a pang. "When?"

"There isn't an actual date," he replies. "I thought it would be when I got better, but I guess I'm just not better enough. Dad says I'll be starting school here."

"Well, in that case, you'll need a bike. I'm not selling; I'm lending. It belongs to my brother."

"Doesn't he need it?" Keenan asks.

"He's away at university," I explain. "Anyway, he drives now, so you can probably just keep it. You know, if your plans change."

"They won't," he promises. He bounces experimentally on the seat. "I feel kind of funny accepting it. I don't have anything to give you."

I fix him with my most engaging grin. "Can you hook me up with a couple of Band-Aids? Some of

46

these scratches are starting to ooze."

That's how I get myself inside the Cardinal house. His place is a lot newer than ours, since it doesn't date back to the gangster days. It's pretty nice. Definitely a bachelor pad, though. Mr. Cardinal lives alone—he wasn't expecting his son to wind up here, except for short visits. All the windows have blinds, period. Not a curtain in the place. And his antiseptic really stings.

"The bike is a must-have," I explain to Keenan as I'm performing first aid on myself. "Centrelight's small, but not *that* small. You're going to need transportation when I show you around the island."

My border officer instincts read his expression perfectly. He's going over our conversation, searching for the place where he signed up for my guided tour. But he's distracted by Barney Two, who has climbed onto the bathroom scale. He weighs fifteen pounds, six ounces. (At home on the Canadian side, that would be seven kilograms.)

"Wait here, Barney—I've got something for you." He disappears into the hall.

"Barney *Two*," I call after him.

He returns a moment later, carrying a small bag of dog treats.

"You don't have a dog," I point out.

"I bought them for this little guy." He offers one to Barney Two.

The spaniel turns to me for approval.

I shrug. "Yeah, sure, whatever. Chow down."

Barney Two inhales the treat, followed by three more.

I apply the last Band-Aid to a nasty cut on my elbow. "All right, I'll be back in ten minutes."

"For what?"

"To run home and get *my* bike," I explain. "The Michigan cops are real sticklers about double-riding."

And when I come back on my own bicycle, Barney Two scrambling at my wheels, there's Keenan on Wayne's bike, waiting for me.

"I called Dr. Sobel," he reports. "He says I'm allowed to ride, so long as I don't overdo it."

Translation: he's a turtle. But that's okay. Life isn't about the destination; it's about enjoying the ride.

There's a lot to see on Centrelight, and I'm the ideal person to show it to Keenan. We start out at Ripley Point on the Canadian side, which is absolutely the best place for throwing rocks. The bluff is forty feet high, so it takes a really long time before you hear the splash. They call it Ripley Point because that's where the gangster Meyer Lansky dumped Reuben Ripley's body when they caught him helping himself to some of the booze shipments to sell for his own profit.

Keenan peers over the cliff to the river far below. "Was Ripley already dead when they threw him over the side?"

"Nobody knows," I reply seriously. "But he definitely was by the time he bounced off those rocks down there. You used to be able to see a red stain on that sharp pointed one, but it's faded over the years."

Keenan frowns. "Cut it out, ZeeBee. There's no way you ever saw blood on those rocks. It was too long ago."

"I'm not saying I saw it," I defend myself. "I'm just saying it used to be there."

I show him stuff on the American side too. The violence was even worse over there. Not only did you have the rival gangs shooting at each other; you also had the FBI trying to arrest everybody before they could run back over into Canada.

"This is the site of the Independence Day Ambush," I tell him with a sweep of my arm.

He looks around, confused. "It's a strip mall."

"It wasn't always a strip mall, dummy. In 1931, the governor of Michigan himself was here for the Fourth of July celebration." I pause for dramatic effect. "So was Al Capone. The official story goes that a stray spark set off all the fireworks before the governor could give the signal. We know better than that, don't we?"

"We do?" Keenan has a habit of raising one eyebrow—the left one. It makes him seem very skeptical.

"There was this crew out of Detroit trying to muscle in on Capone's business here in Centrelight. So just as people were finishing up their hot dogs, one of Capone's guys tossed a lit match into the fireworks. A half-hour display went off in, like, thirty seconds. There was a lot of noise, so nobody noticed a few extra booms, pops, and bangs in there. But when it was all over, the entire Detroit crew was scattered around the park, dead. Pretty cool, huh?"

"I guess," he replies dubiously. "If you think murder is cool."

"Hey," I put in quickly, "I'm not saying being a gangster is okay. I'm totally on the law-and-order side. My own father is a lawman."

"Well—a border officer—"

"That's a lawman," I insist. "Last week, he caught this lady who bought an eight-thousand-dollar wedding dress in Detroit and was trying to bring it into

Canada without paying import duty. If that's not law and order, I don't know what is!"

Keenan doesn't seem all that impressed. His attention wanders to Barney Two, who is nuzzling an extra-large dandelion that has sprouted through a crack in the sidewalk. The door of the food market opens and Mr. Chaiken rushes out with a long-handled broom. He takes a home-run swing and sweeps Barney Two right off the pavement. "Get away from here," he hollers. "And keep your horrible dog with you!"

Keenan jumps off his bike and scoops Barney Two protectively into his arms. "You'll hurt him!" he complains.

"I won't touch a hair on his little haunch—so long as he stays out of my place of business," the shopkeeper exclaims heatedly. "It's her fault!" Now the broom is pointing in my direction. "She trained her other dog to barge into the store and eat all my cheese!"

"I didn't *train* him," I say with dignity. "Barney liked cheese."

"He'd hide behind the dumpster"—the grocer's voice shakes with fury—"waiting for a customer to open the automatic door. Then he'd pounce. By the time I caught up to him, half the cheese case would be gone. Cheddar, Gouda, Brie—he was into it all. Even when he left some, how could I sell it? He cost me thousands. And go make an insurance claim? They laughed in my face!"

"This isn't the same dog, mister!" Keenan shouts. "This one wouldn't mess with your cheese."

"He hasn't got the moxie," I add, missing my Barney more than ever.

Mr. Chaiken scowls at me. "I'm supposed to trust you? You raised one monster, you can raise another. Just because this one looks sweet and quiet means nothing. I have to protect my livelihood." He storms back inside his shop, the automatic door whooshing shut behind him.

I shrug. "I told you everyone hated Barney."

Barney Two wriggles out of Keenan's arms and trots over to rub against my sneaker.

"That guy's a jerk!" Keenan exclaims angrily. "How would he like it if we spread the word that he attacks defenseless little dogs? I'll bet no one would shop at his 'livelihood' then."

I shake my head. "They wouldn't care. They remember Barney, and nobody liked him any better than Mr. Chaiken did. That's why I haven't figured out who the killer is yet, because the whole island had a motive to hurt him."

"Unless your parents are right and he really *did* die from old age," Keenan reminds me.

I don't answer, because he's got that eyebrow up again, so no matter what I say, he won't believe it anyway. Besides, I don't know Keenan that well yet, and I refuse to show him how sad I am.

It's not so much the fact that Barney's gone. I'm used to that. It's the fact that I'm the only one who misses him.

5

Keenan

Sometimes I feel guilty that I only hang out with ZeeBee to play with Barney Two. I know that sounds bad. I mean, I really do like ZeeBee. But her cocker spaniel happens to be the sweetest, smartest little guy on earth. For sure, he's entitled to some actual human affection. And he definitely isn't getting that from his owner.

If there's one good thing about contracting TB and having to leave my life in China to come recover on this weird island in the middle of nowhere, it's Barney Two. Poor pup—he doesn't even have a real name, just a holdover from the Godzilla of all dogs.

"You know what would be the perfect name for him?" I say, tossing the tennis ball, which Barney Two leaps up and snaps out of the air. "Lancelot. Like the knight. Lance for short."

She looks at me like I'm crazy. "He's named after the greatest dog that ever lived!"

We're walking along St. Clair Avenue in the middle of downtown. It's the part where the border is so zigzaggy that you can be in a different country practically every few steps. As we talk, I'm throwing the ball to Barney Two, who's snatching it out of the air and bringing it back to me, loving the game. Although he's playing with me, he keeps looking at ZeeBee for approval and getting none. That's how starved he is for her attention.

"How about Rocket?" I suggest, still working on dog names.

She snorts. "He wouldn't rocket if you filled his water dish with jet fuel."

"What are you talking about? Look at his vertical leap!"

To prove my point, I lob the ball high over Barney

Two's head. He leaps for it, missing by only a couple of inches, and then takes off in pursuit as it bounces along the street. It ricochets off the sign advertising the Centerlight Mob Museum and drops down a few cement steps to the building's basement entrance. Barney Two dashes after it. I'm right behind him. ZeeBee brings up the rear.

Barney Two surrenders the ball after the usual tug-of-war. He loses interest in me, though, when ZeeBee taps on the museum window. "Check it out."

I peer inside. It's a plain white room with a primitive piece of wooden furniture, dead center.

"An old chair?" I ask ZeeBee.

"Look closer."

I press my face against the glass. "My grandmother has one like that. Guaranteed to give you a backache if you spend too much time on it."

"Believe me," ZeeBee replies gravely. "Nobody spends too much time in this one. Think about what this place is. The *mob* museum?"

"All right, I give up. What's it supposed to be?"

"How many chairs do you know with leg straps and a helmet."

I gawk. "Is that—an *electric* chair?"

"Bingo," she confirms proudly. "Eliot Ness brought it here personally. Why waste it in some federal prison when most of the people who needed executing were right here on the island?"

I feel myself turning green. "How many?"

"Forty-seven," she replies immediately. "Can you imagine their electric bill? But at least they saved gas not having to drive guys down to Joliet."

I shoot her a skeptical glance.

Her earnest expression never wavers. "Well, maybe not forty-seven. More like twenty-two. At least ten," she adds. "And maybe Eliot Ness had it shipped."

I never know quite what to make of ZeeBee's stories. On the one hand, she has to be at least a little bit full of it. On the other, she's such a natural storyteller that it's like the normal standard of true versus made-up doesn't apply to her. The story is all that matters, so she twists the facts to make it as good as it can be. Is that so terrible? It wasn't terrible when I was stuck on a lawn chair in the backyard with a dead phone, and her company was the only thing that kept me from losing my mind. Besides her, I have exactly zero friends on the island. To be honest, I didn't think I'd need any. But now it looks like that's going to change. Like it or not, I'm here for the foreseeable future.

"Let's go someplace else," I say. "That thing creeps me out."

ZeeBee shrugs. "Don't blame a Canadian. You're the ones who used the chair. We just hanged people. Want to see where the gallows used to be?"

I shudder. "No, thanks."

"Then how about some fro-yo?"

That's another thing about ZeeBee. She can switch topics from gallows to frozen yogurt in the blink of an eye. It's a good quality, I think. Hanging out with her can be exhausting when it's all gangster executions and pet murder without anything lighter to balance it out.

The dessert place is a couple of blocks away on the Canadian side. While we're eating, I show ZeeBee some of the pictures on my phone. Every photo has kind of a backstory to it. Like the shot of me two years ago falling on my face during the dance-off at my school in Lesotho.

ZeeBee points to the girl trying to moonwalk beside me. "Who's she?"

"Sumaiya," I reply. "Monster volleyball player. Her dad was the ambassador from Bangladesh."

"Bangladesh?" she echoes. "You lived there too?"

I shake my head. "All the diplomats' kids go to international school, so you've got friends from pretty much everywhere. The families from my school in Shanghai spoke over two hundred languages."

It's kind of fun to be doing some of the talking for a change. When you hang out with ZeeBee, it's tough to get a word in edgewise.

She stares at my sixth-grade class picture until I realize that her interest isn't so much in the kids as the location. Our school trip last year was to the Great Wall of China, and the photo was taken on top of it, in front of one of those guard towers. In the background you can see the ramparts going on and on forever.

"Man," she breathes. "Can you imagine if our border looked like that? I never would have met you."

"Life would definitely be different if we had to climb over that every time we wanted to cross the street," I agree with a snicker.

"Or use the bathroom at the post office," she adds seriously.

It's all I can do to keep from cracking up as I picture little Centerlight with a giant fortified wall twisting down the middle, slicing through lawns and the bowling alley, separating Taco Bell from its parking lot, and cutting the lighthouse in two.

She flips back in the gallery and brings up a shot from when we lived in Korea—nine-year-old me during my orange belt test in tae kwon do.

ZeeBee laughs at my expense. "Check out those pajamas!" She looks a little closer. "Hey, you could really fly."

"Pre-tuberculosis," I explain glumly, thinking of my training sessions at Island Fitness. I'm doing okay on the weights. Still, I get out of breath way too easily. "I'm not hitting that kick anytime soon. Bryce says I should be patient, but I'm not sure I'll ever get back to where I was."

She makes a face. "That guy needs a personality transplant. I see him around town a lot, flexing. Does he even know how to smile? Or did he transfer all his facial muscles to his pecs?"

"He smiles," I say defensively. I'm trying to come up with specific examples when her expression abruptly turns grim. I follow her eyes to the front door. A kid is coming into the shop—a boy about our age.

"What?" I whisper.

She's tight-lipped.

He comes over. "Hi, *Zarabeth*." It's a greeting and it's not. He stretches out the name. His gaze travels to me. "Hey, kid."

"Keenan," ZeeBee supplies.

"One of yours?" he questions.

She shakes her head. "One of *yours*, Ronnie. He lives with his dad over on Sequoia."

"No kidding." Ronnie looks at me, minus the sneer. "I guess I'll be seeing you around school."

It takes me a second to catch up to what they're talking about. "One of yours" means that this Ronnie kid and I are both *American*.

"Yeah, guess so." Something tells me not to invite him to join us at our table.

He nods in the direction of Barney Two, who's tied up just outside. "That your new dog?"

"It's *a* dog," ZeeBee deadpans.

"His name is Barney Two," I put in.

Ronnie grins. "Did you ever meet Barney One? You'd definitely remember."

ZeeBee has been looking anywhere except at Ronnie. Now she wheels and fixes him with a glare that packs the power of the electric chair across the street.

Ronnie doesn't take the bait. "Well, good meeting you, Keenan. Later, *Zarabeth*." He buys a vanilla flying saucer at the counter, and exits the store. As he passes Barney Two, he pats him on the head, because he knows it'll annoy ZeeBee.

"You don't like that guy," I comment.

"His dad used to call the cops on Barney," she complains. "His family even tried to sue us once when their poodle had these really funny-looking puppies. The webbed feet were a dead giveaway. It wasn't just cheese, you know. Barney had all kinds of interests."

I make a face. "This guy Ronnie must be a real jerk if he holds it against you."

She shrugs. "That's not it. I mean, Ronnie's an idiot, but he isn't any worse than all the other idiots around here. The problem is I don't go to *school* with them. That's who your friends are—the people you see in class, the ones you're with every day. I get on the ferry and go to the mainland to school. And I don't make friends there either, because as soon as the day's done, I'm back on the boat and gone."

Wow, I never thought about it like that. ZeeBee's in a tough spot, being an islander in every way but one. It's easy to overlook, because here, nobody really notices which side of the border you come from. But what school you go to—that's a huge part of your life. No wonder ZeeBee didn't laugh at the idea of the Great Wall of China cutting Centerlight in two. In her world, that invisible line might as well be a giant physical barrier. So what if she can cross it whenever she wants to? In every way that matters, she's permanently stuck on one side of it.

That explains why she kept coming back to me, a guy who was sentenced to hard time in his dad's backyard. I wasn't going to tell her she wasn't part of the club. I didn't know what the club *was*.

I try to cheer her up. "Well, what am I, chopped liver? *We're* friends, right?"

Her mood isn't rebounding. "Just wait. You'll probably go to school with Ronnie and those morons and forget all about me."

"You never forget the person who introduces you to your first electric chair," I tease.

She pushes her frozen yogurt away, half-finished. "You'll see."

Dad has to take me to register on the first day of school—like I'm in kindergarten or something. The only other first-timers really *are* in kindergarten, so I look like a total idiot, standing in line with all those blubbering five-year-olds. The little kid next to us alternates between sobbing and negotiating with his mom over how many Power Rangers she promises to buy him if he goes to school "like a big boy." She's offered two; he's angling for four.

"All right. How many Power Rangers is this going to cost me?" Dad asks me with a wink. "Or Pokémon? Thomas trains?"

Dad thinks he's hilarious. He's alone in this.

"I used to have Power Rangers," I inform him, deadpan. "Chinese customs confiscated them. They were culturally subversive."

Dad sighs. Mom's globe-trotting gets on his nerves. He just doesn't understand the expat life. Most Americans don't. And if ZeeBee is any hint, Canadians don't either.

The population of Centerlight doesn't change much. Most island kids are born here. Newcomers are rare. So when I explain that, in order to get my school records, the office is going to have to contact countries like China, Hungary, and Brazil, I get a lot of strange looks. The assistant principal, Mr. Federle, accuses me of making up Lesotho.

"Well, it seems like everything's under control here," Dad announces after the Lesotho incident. "I should probably hit the road to get into the city before my office realizes they can get along without me."

I stare at him in dismay. When he was selling Mom and me on the move to Centerlight for my recovery, he said a lot of encouraging things like *I'm your parent too* and *Don't worry, I've got your back as long as you're living under my roof.* Did that only count when I was lying like a rock in the yard? And now that I'm still alive, I'm on my own?

As the secretary leads me out of the office to my period-one class, we pass Mr. Federle. He's staring at Africa on a globe, probably trying to find Lesotho. I hope it's there. That globe looks pretty old.

"It's completely landlocked by South Africa," I explain helpfully.

He gives me a dirty look.

The good news is that geometry isn't any different in Centerlight than it is in Shanghai. The school part is stable, even if my living situation isn't.

It's kind of awkward. One advantage of international schools is there's no such thing as being the new guy, because *everybody*'s the new guy. Diplomats get reassigned, the global business crowd follows fresh opportunities, and people like Mom and Klaus take new jobs in different countries because they love experiencing new cultures and places. And when the adults move, their kids move with them. But my classmates here have been together since Centerlight Gymboree. It's not that they're mean—they aren't. Even that Ronnie kid from the frozen yogurt place says hi when he sees me. It's just that they have their long-established groups and cliques and I don't belong to any of them.

At lunch in the cafeteria, I sit at the end of a long table. I'm not alone—in fact, the place is packed. But I might as well be all by myself. I pick at my sweet-and-sour pork with a pair of wooden chopsticks that are 90 percent splinters—in Shanghai, they would be banned by the government as lethal weapons.

That's when a voice at my elbow exclaims, "Man, how do you do that?"

I look up in surprise. After being completely ignored all morning, I'm suddenly the center of attention.

"Do what?" I ask. "Eat lunch?"

"Yeah, but the chopsticks!" the kid persists.

"They're awful," I agree. "I'm getting more wood than food."

A girl breaks in. "How do you pick up the smaller pieces? I always drop everything."

I frown. "Haven't you guys ever seen chopsticks before?"

Ronnie speaks up. "Of course we have. But they slow down the very important process of food getting into my mouth." He stabs at a piece of pork and it sails over his shoulder and hits the floor, to laughter and some sarcastic applause.

I survey the table. A lot of kids are having sweet-and-sour pork, which is the hot food option on today's lunch. But I'm the only one attempting it with chopsticks. Where I come from, Chinese food is just called food, and chopsticks are the delivery system. Up and down the table, kids are eating with plastic forks and even shoveling with spoons. The only chopsticks in action are being used for sword fighting.

I take another bite. Every pair of eyes follows the piece of meat from the plate to my mouth. I almost choke.

Ronnie snaps apart a pair of chopsticks. "Okay, expert, why don't you show us."

That's how I end up walking up and down the long table, giving chopsticks lessons, straightening fingers and adjusting kids' techniques. Mr. Federle comes up to me, ready to chew me out. It's like he doesn't know what I'm doing, but he's pretty sure it's against the rules. He stops short and watches me show Carla Harouni how to hold the top stick between her middle finger and the base of her thumb. She's kind of clumsy, but she's getting better, practicing on a bowl of grapes. Her friend Gabrielle Beckham has the fingering right, but she's pressing so hard that she crushes everything she picks up. A puddle of grape juice is forming in front of them.

"This how they eat in Lesotho?" the assistant principal asks.

"Shanghai," I reply. "But at the schools I went to, most kids were good with chopsticks because they'd lived all over."

He walks away, shaking his head.

Ronnie grins up at me. "Man, you sure schooled Federle."

"I don't think he likes me very much," I say.

"Don't take it personally," Joey Cobretti assures me. "Federle hates everybody."

That turns out to be sort of my official welcome to Centerlight Middle School. If Mr. Federle thinks I'm worth hating, then I must be okay.

I don't know how popular I'm going to be with the lunchroom staff, though. After forty minutes of chopsticks lessons—beginner level—the table looks like a war zone. But at my next class, social studies, Ronnie and Joey save me a seat between them.

"So," Ronnie whispers as we wait for the teacher to arrive, "what's up with you and Zoo-doo?"

"Zoo-doo?" I echo.

"You know—*Zarabeth*." He stretches the name out the way he did in the fro-yo place that day. "She your girlfriend or something?"

"Of course not!" I exclaim. "She's just the first kid I met on the island." I give a quick recap of how Zee-Bee found me during one of those long afternoons fumigating my TB germs in Dad's backyard. "Why do you call her Zoo-doo?"

"It's this fancy fertilizer my mom uses in her vegetable garden," Joey supplies. "Made from the poop of zoo animals. You know—ZeeBee, Zoo-doo."

"That girl's weird, man," Ronnie adds.

"She's not so bad," I say. "It can't be easy, going to that school on the mainland when everybody else comes here. It's like you're odd man out before you've even started."

Ronnie shakes his head. "That doesn't explain everything. You ever talk to Zoo-doo? The gangster stuff? She's crazy."

"She's pretty into island history," I concede. "And her family lives in a famous gangster house."

"All that was a long time ago," Joey scoffs. "It's just for the tourists now. Like you can go to the O.K. Corral on vacation, but don't expect to meet Wyatt Earp in the hot tub."

I start to say, "She knows that—" but the protest dies in my throat. I remember ZeeBee's exact words:

Things happen here. She spoke of mysterious footprints and voices. *Someone's watching our house, Keenan,* she told me. *I'd swear to it.*

Does that sound like someone who understands that Centerlight's gangster past is exactly that—in the past?

"She thinks somebody killed that giant mutt of hers," Ronnie adds. "Next thing you know, she'll say it was Al Capone."

"Her new dog's pretty nice," I put in, a little guilty that I don't have more to offer in ZeeBee's defense. On the other hand, Ronnie and Joey haven't said anything I don't agree with yet. They could be nicer about it, but I totally get how other kids would see her that way.

"Yeah, well, she owes us a nice one," Ronnie retorts. "She owes us fifty nice ones after Barney. Listen, Keenan, we all cried when Old Yeller died, but I guarantee you nobody shed a tear for that monster."

"ZeeBee never said that Barney was *good*," I point out. "Just that she loved him."

"Hooray for her," Joey puts in bitterly. "That dog was the nastiest thing ever to set foot on Centerlight, and I include the old-time gangsters on that list. My mom's precious garden—Barney used to trash it twice a week. You put up a fence—he goes under, or over, or through. You stand guard and spray him with the hose—he bites you. You call the cops—well, they're scared of him too."

At that point, Mrs. Prager breezes in, officially ending our conversation. I try to picture ZeeBee at her own school on the Canadian mainland. I feel bad that she's not here to speak up for herself. Still, most of what I heard from Ronnie and Joey I've already heard from ZeeBee herself. She's the one who talked about how terrible Barney was, and how much everybody hated him.

It's amazing how everything seems different when you look at it from another perspective.

6

Zarabeth

The eighteen-minute ferry ride from Corunna on the mainland to Centrelight might as well be an ocean crossing. It's a bright, sunny day, but you can't tell by the passengers on the deck. We're suffocating in the black cloud that billows out of the smokestack and swirls all around us. It's still better than going belowdecks. That's where the little kids hang out with their mothers and nannies who escort them to and from school. You can't even imagine the noise. When you're that age, there's only one volume setting (eleven). Whether they're laughing, crying, or describing the high and low points of their day, the screaming never stops. Even up here, over the thrum of the engine, you can still hear the squeals.

I'm the only non–high schooler on deck, so nobody pays any attention to me. There seem to be a lot of couples this year. I give that about five minutes. The ferry ride is usually the place for some spectacular breakups, but this is only the first day. A lot of relationships bit the dust on that day last April when the ferry lost power, and we floated for three hours before the tugboat came. And even then it was kind of an international incident, because it was an American tugboat rescuing a Canadian ferry.

Grade Seven. Yawn. Every September, the teachers tell us how the party's over and how serious everything is going to get, so we have to "buckle down." But so far, Grade Seven looks a lot like a reboot of Grade Six, with everybody a year older.

Big surprise, we have to write about something that happened during summer vacation. I'm going to do my paper on Keenan and how I helped him recover from tuberculosis. Keenan is really interesting because he's lived in all these cool places. Which is great except for the getting tuberculosis part.

The thing is Keenan hasn't told me that much about the countries he's lived in other than the fact that he's lived there. And the international schools don't sound so special except for where they're located. His friends over there sound exactly like the kind of kids you could meet here. So-and-so who memorized almost every single rap lyric; so-and-so who was on the swim team, or the track team, or the robotics team; so-and-so who Keenan went with to tae kwon do class. You don't have to fly to distant continents to find that. There isn't even anybody on the list as interesting as, let's say, someone who lives in a house that used to belong to a notorious gangster.

Anyway, when Keenan and I hang out together, I usually do most of the talking. After all, when I first knew him, he would get out of breath easily. That's not true anymore, but when friends set up a pattern like that, it sticks. Plus, at the beginning, Keenan knew nothing about the history of Centrelight and all the gangsters who used to operate here. You can't blame Keenan and me if people like Al Capone and Tommy-Gun Ferguson are a lot more exciting than a bunch of random cities around the globe.

As we cross the river, I'm tempted to call ahead and

let him know I'm on the way. The problem is it's an international long-distance call, even though he lives only a few blocks from my house. And my phone is on a Canadian plan, so talking to the United States costs two dollars a minute, even though you could probably yell there for free, or even stretch a string between two tin cans. It's Dad's fault—he has to use a Canadian carrier for work. And with my brother, Wayne, in Toronto, it just makes sense. But two dollars a minute can really add up—especially when you have as much to say as I do. And when that big bill comes in, do you think Dad appreciates the impossible situation he's put me in? No, he confiscates my phone. It's a border officer thing. They just can't stop confiscating stuff. It's a compulsion.

So the phone stays in my pocket, and the eighteen minutes passes like eighteen years. Finally, we make it to Centrelight, where the red maple leaf of Canada flies over the lighthouse—it's Tuesday, our day. The wharf lets us out into Laurier Park, which turns into Jefferson Park where the border bisects it, about halfway through.

I head straight for Keenan's house, but I haven't left the park yet when a voice hails me. "ZeeBee! Over here!"

I wheel. There are a lot of kids in the park—the middle school is just over the rise. A sprawling game of Frisbee is under way, the spinning disc crossing an international frontier on almost every throw. And in the middle of it, jumping up and down and waving, is Keenan.

I'm confused for an instant, although actually, it makes perfect sense. He spent all day at school, same as I did. But he didn't have to leave his classmates back on the mainland. They're all right here in the park, hanging out and having a great time. I can't help experiencing a stab of disappointment. A week ago, I was the only person on Centrelight he knew.

Bummer, but I should have seen it coming. It's not like *that* was going to last.

As I start to jog over, the Frisbee comes sailing at Keenan. The throw is off target—high and to the left. But somehow, he takes off in a spectacular leap, his legs splayed out in a near-split. He makes the catch with the tip of a finger before crashing to the grass.

Keenan's still for a moment. Then his arm shoots up, holding the Frisbee in triumph. Not bad for a guy who was laid out with TB just a couple of weeks ago. I can kind of see the junior tae kwon do master he used to be. It's probably only a matter of time before he nails that kick in his training sessions with Creepy Musclehead.

The others mob him and haul him to his feet in a blizzard of backslaps and high fives. That's when I start to recognize people. That jerk Ronnie and this kid Joey he hangs out with. Carla's there, and this girl Gabrielle—we used to be best friends as little kids but grew apart when I started going to school on the mainland. More faces come into view. Ethan—his mother swung a snow shovel at Barney once. I'll bet the teeth marks are still in the scoop. Lisette—she had her bat mitzvah this past spring, and I was the only girl on the island our age who didn't get invited. Her uncle called the cops on us once because Barney messed with the tow hitch on his truck and unhooked his motorboat trailer. He had to drop the charges, though, because nobody could figure out which court to take us to. Even though the boat was parked in the United States, by the time it rolled down the hill and hit that tree, it had crossed into Canada.

I see kids I went to preschool with; kids who now barely glance in my direction when I pass them on the street.

"ZeeBee!" Keenan calls again.

I execute a 180 and get out of there, pretending I

don't hear him. There's a lump in my throat that I can't quite explain. I always knew he was going to meet other people. I just kept myself from admitting it would be *those* people.

Ignoring him, I leave the park and turn onto my street. Our house is kind of unique. Tommy-Gun Ferguson built a little cupola on the roof so he could post a guard to look out for police and rival gangsters. Sometimes I sit up there and survey the neighborhood just in case not all of those gangsters are in the past. I *know* people have been skulking around our house, whether Dad believes me or not. We really should have surveillance cameras, but Dad's too cheap. I was saving up to buy some on my own, but it turns out they're more expensive than I thought.

Anyway, if you can't afford cameras, a good lookout spot is the next best thing. I was going to show it to Keenan one day soon. I wonder if that's ever going to happen now.

I enter the house and practically trip over Barney Two, who's waiting just inside the door.

"He's been sitting there ever since you left this morning," my mother makes a point of informing me.

I see what she's up to. She's judging me. She thinks I have to love this dog just because he's dumb enough to love me for no reason. Well, it won't work. Already his yipping and wagging is getting on my nerves, and I've only been home for ten seconds.

"If that was the real Barney," I say belligerently, "he would have busted down that door instead of waiting for me to come through it. *He* had character."

"I remember," Mum returns. "If Barney had a little less character, this family would have a lot less debt."

She's thinking about the fines. We had to pay those, since Barney obviously didn't have any money. Or she might mean the dog food bill, which wasn't small. I think Mr. Chaiken overcharged us. We bought our kibble in the same place Barney went hunting for cheese.

I'm not in the mood to argue, so I grab an apple and head up to the cupola to be by myself. I might as well get used to it. And anyway, I can't even manage that. Barney Two follows me there, his little toenails clicking on the metal steps. The real Barney never made any noise approaching a click. With him, it was either a resounding *thwomp* or nothing.

"Go away," I say listlessly.

His tail wags even faster.

I do some homework on my iPad, but I can't finish because the internet connection keeps cutting out on me. That's Tommy-Gun Ferguson for you—great at killing people; not so good at building a house for reliable Wi-Fi. I've been there about an hour when I spot Keenan heading down our street. A moment later, I hear the doorbell, followed by Mum's voice.

"ZeeBee—your friend is on his way up."

I'm actually annoyed. I was planning to show him the cupola eventually, but on *my* schedule. And then he's tackling the metal stairs, his school bag on his shoulders, his cheeks red with exertion. Which means he hasn't been home yet. He's come straight from the park where he's been all this time. With *them*.

"Hey, ZeeBee. I saw you getting off the ferry. Didn't you hear me?"

"Yeah, well," I say, "I don't go where I'm not wanted."

"What do you mean, not wanted?" he retorts. "You were wanted. I was calling you."

"*You* were calling. One person out of twenty."

He shrugs. "They're my friends. They can be your friends too."

Friends. One day at that school and Keenan has friends. "You don't have to introduce us," I remind him. "I was born here, and so were most of them."

"Aw, ZeeBee, don't be like that. They're not so bad.

I've been all over the world. Kids are the same every-where."

Suddenly, I need to change the subject. "Check out this view, eh? Tommy-Gun Ferguson built this cupola—he called it his 'lookout tower.'"

Keenan elevates that brow. "I guess it didn't work out too well. He got arrested, right?"

I nod. "Your lookout tower is only as good as your lookout. The guy cut a deal with the FBI to save him-self from going to prison."

The brow rises even farther. I feel like I'm the one on trial, not Tommy-Gun.

"Or so I've heard," I add.

The brow comes down again.

"Anyway," I go on, "that was it for Tommy-Gun. When the feds kicked the door in, there was no time to get to the hidey-hole."

Keenan's intrigued. "There's a hidey-hole?"

"Yeah. You want to see it?"

"It's just that—you said he had a big stash of gold and nobody ever found it."

"I thought of that years ago," I tell him. "The hidey-hole is just a trapdoor in the back of a closet. Barney claimed it, but he thought it was a toilet. We had to shovel it out every couple of days. Dad wasn't a big fan of that, let me tell you. Anyway, the only thing you'll find there now is Wayne's old hockey equipment. No gold."

I can see he's hooked, so I give him a tour of the house, Barney Two at our heels. I might get a little too creative about the gangster connection. For example, that brown spot on the kitchen counter could be where Dutch Schultz once stubbed out a cigar, but it could have been a bunch of other things too. All we know for sure is it won't come off, not even with CLR.

His eyes practically bug out of his head when the fireplace tools on the hearth catch the sunlight and gleam yellow gold.

"Brass," I explain. "Mum got them from eBay a couple of months ago. Most of our stuff didn't come with the house. But"—I point to a large framed map of Centrelight on the wall opposite the fireplace—"that was here when we moved in." I lead him over to stand in front of it.

"You think it belonged to Tommy-Gun?" he asks.

"Not originally," I reply. "It's from the 1880s—even before *his* time. You see a few of these around town—the first official map of the island after Canada and the United States decided where the border was going to be."

"Pretty cool," he comments.

"Yeah, cool."

This isn't the first time I've stared at that squiggly line that looks like a dizzy ant staggered his way across the paper.

That line is the reason why Keenan has a full roster of friends after only a few hours at school, and I've got only him.

7

Ronnie

I like the new kid. Keenan is pretty cool—and is there a place he hasn't lived yet? Antarctica? Mars? He's got skills with a Frisbee. He knows how to put teachers in their place too. I don't know what he's thinking hanging out with Zoo-doo, but nobody's perfect. He just got here. He'll learn.

Besides, the best thing about the new kid is that he's new. When you grow up on an island like Centerlight, you get so sick of looking at the same old faces day after day, week after week, month after month, year after year. I'd include decade after decade, but I won't be here that long. There isn't a single thing that you don't already know about every solitary soul that you meet on this rock. That's why somebody new is like Christmas and the Fourth of July all rolled into one.

Like Keenan's iPhone is a little different from my iPhone since it was made for the Chinese market. That doesn't sound like much, but I didn't know that! I've spent so much time staring at Joey's phone that I've memorized every spiderweb-like screen crack. Not Keenan's, which, in addition to being in perfect condition, also has Chinese writing under the Apple logo on the back.

Keenan will be going back to China when he's done getting better from TB. When that day comes, it's impossible to say how I'll feel about it. The last time we had a new kid around here, I was about six. We get summer people on the island, but I'm always away at camp during the summer, so who cares?

Keenan lives with his dad. His mom is still in China. That sounds like a nice deal to me. It means she can't stick her nose into his life every time the wind blows. My mom could sure learn a thing or two from that.

Unfortunately, it doesn't work that way with moms. The first time I'm over at Keenan's house, he gets Skyped all the way from Shanghai.

"Hi, sweetie!" comes a woman's voice over the computer. "How are you feeling?"

Sweetie? OMG, it's a good thing Keenan's going back to China, because I'm never going to let him hear the end of that! What's next? Snookums? Honey-bunches?

"Fine," he replies. "Dad and I are getting along great, and I've started school here."

The voice becomes suspicious. "You sound out of breath."

That's because he's trying not to laugh. I'm behind his computer, making faces and lip-synching everything his mom says. He picks up a pen and throws it at me. I duck and it bounces off the wall, leaving a blue mark.

"Don't worry," he assures her. "Dr. Sobel says I'm not contagious anymore. I'm going to a trainer to build up my strength. I'm even making a few friends."

You can tell that's not what she wants to hear. If Keenan's having a normal life here, maybe he won't want to go back to China. That wouldn't work with me—I'd go to the moon if it would get me off Centerlight!

I get bored with their conversation and begin to rifle through his closet. Using the pen he threw at me, I pick up a pair of tightie-whities and wave them like a flag of surrender. I dangle them over my open mouth like a sword swallower. Man, I hope this isn't his dirty laundry.

By now, Keenan is snickering, and his mom is getting annoyed. "Well, if you don't have time for me, sweetie—"

"*Sweetie,*" I echo in a singsong tone.

"No!" Keenan's babbling now. "It's just that, uh, I've got this, uh, homework—" And with a few more apologies and sweeties, they're off the line.

"Get away from my underwear," he snaps at me.

I drop the briefs but continue to dig through the closet. "What are you, sweetie, one of those monks who renounces all earthly possessions? You've got no stuff!"

"I've got stuff," he defends himself. "In Shanghai. This isn't my room; it's my dad's guest room. Remember, when I came here, the only thing I brought with me was TB and a toothbrush."

I hold up a T-shirt covered in Chinese characters, with the Pepsi logo at the bottom. "What does this say?"

He laughs. "It's kind of a joke. It was supposed to be 'Come alive with the Pepsi generation.' But it actually translates more like 'Pepsi brings your ancestors back from the grave.' It's a big hit in Shanghai. Anyway, how can you say I've got nothing? What about this?"

He holds up a cheap souvenir keychain featuring Al Capone on one side and Eliot Ness on the other. It's one of the top sellers for visitors who come to Centerlight for that gangster garbage. Of all the things I'm sick of about this dumb island, that has to be number one.

I make a face at him. "Tourist junk."

"I didn't buy it," he tells me. "ZeeBee got it for me."

I shake my head in disgust. "Figures. Zoo-doo sees a gangster under every rock."

"Don't call her that."

"Fine—*Zarabeth*."

"Don't call her that either."

"It's her name, isn't it?" I challenge.

"I mean don't say it that way. She's smart. Funny. And she hung out with me when I couldn't do anything more than lie like a rock on a lounge chair."

"I never said she's a bad person," I point out. "I just said she's weird. You've got to give me that. And that *dog*—"

"The dog's out of the picture," he reminds me.

"Yeah, I know. *Murdered.*"

"Okay, that part *is* weird," he concedes. "But you barely know ZeeBee—"

"Are you kidding?" I cut him off. "I've known her since we were babies."

"Fine, then you should give her a second chance. Everybody should."

"Yeah, whatever." That annoys me. Who does he think he is, my parents? He's got to learn how things work around here.

Which gives me an idea . . .

"Hey, drop by my place tonight. I'll invite a few friends over."

He brightens. "You mean like a party?"

"More like a hangout. My dad's away on business, so it should be a blast. Everything's better when he's not around."

"What about your mom?"

"She won't bother us," I assure him. "She's not too big on confrontation."

"I'll ask my father," he promises.

Just because we live in the most boring place on earth doesn't mean we don't know how to have a good time. Just the opposite—we have to try twice as hard as everybody else, since Centerlight is so lame.

Once Keenan has some fun in a non–Zoo-doo setting, he'll get the picture.

8

Keenan

onnie Lindahl's house is a pretty good hike from mine—clear on the other side of downtown, on the opposite shore of the river. I could probably make it on my own, but Dad insists on driving.

"You know, two months ago, I was riding the Shanghai Metro on my own," I inform him from the passenger seat. "I took trains to visit friends all around a city with more people than New York and Chicago combined."

His knuckles whiten on the steering wheel. "I wish you hadn't told me that."

"It's totally cool," I insist. "Everyone uses public transportation over there. It's the best way to get around."

He sighs. "Fair enough. But *here*, a man's allowed to give his own son a ride without being overprotective, okay?" He turns onto Shore Road. "I spoke to Bryce over at the gym. He said you're doing amazing, but you tend to push yourself too hard. Something about a karate kick?"

"Tae kwon do," I correct. "If I could land it when I was nine, why am I having so much trouble with it now if I'm supposed to be so 'amazing'?"

"Have some patience," he advises. "You were really sick, Keenan. I know you feel better now, and that's good news. But it's going to take a long time before you're a hundred percent again." He pulls up in front of the Lindahl house and whistles. "Nice place."

It isn't a mansion, exactly, but the house is impressive, at the center of a large, well-landscaped property. You can see the water beyond a fenced-in yard, and, across the river, the wooded shoreline of Michigan, shrouded in dusk.

I thank Dad for the ride and jump out. Nobody

answers the door, so I head out around to the back. As I make my way, I start to hear hip-hop music and notice the glow of what might be a bonfire. There's no small amount of noise, but I can't see over the fence, which is six feet high. I'm searching for a gate when I come to a section where the wooden slats are smashed and missing. There's plenty of room for me to duck right through into the yard.

The first person I meet is Joey, who greets me with, "Hey, look who decided to show up!"

I survey the property. There are at least twenty kids here already, hanging out in groups, roasting hot dogs and marshmallows over the firepit, and dancing on a stone patio. I guess this is what Ronnie means by inviting "a few friends over."

Ronnie appears. "Sweetie—glad you could make it!"

I grimace. "Next time my mom Skypes in, remind me to kick you out."

Joey indicates the hole in the fence. "Keenan found the secret entrance."

"Yeah, what happened?" I ask.

Ronnie shrugs. "What do you think? Zoo-doo's dog."

"Barney did *that*?" I'm blown away. "A rhino, maybe. But a *dog*?"

"My folks had a barbecue," Ronnie explains. "Big mistake. The monster had a thing for porterhouse." He nods in the direction of the breach.

It's an eye-opener for me. I've already heard a lot from ZeeBee about the damage Barney did around the island. This is a solid wooden fence and he came through it like a bulldozer, snapping the slats like they were uncooked spaghetti.

"Well, at least it can't happen again," I point out. "Barney's gone now."

"Gone but not forgotten," Ronnie agrees. "My dad'll have it fixed. You know, when golf season's over."

"Well, anyway," I say, "great party."

Ronnie skewers me with a sharp glance. "It's not a party, sweetie."

I look around. More kids are arriving every minute. "What else would you call it?"

"Ronnie's banned from having parties," Joey supplies. "Call it what you like—call it Harold. But if the P-word comes up, things are going to get ugly when Mr. Lindahl gets back from his trip."

Ronnie runs off to play host, so Joey drags me to the firepit. We roast hot dogs over the flames. By the time I put away two of them, I'm having a pretty good night. I recognize just about everybody from some class or other. But meeting them here, in a non-school setting, kind of cements the fact that I'm fitting in.

I've been to parties before—excuse me, *Harolds*—but nothing quite like this. For one thing, most international schools are in big cities. People live in apartments, and not even the rich kids have this much space. But mostly, when you're overseas, there's always a feeling that you're a guest in someone else's country. You can have fun, maybe even break the occasional rule, but you're sort of on your best behavior. Not here. On Centerlight, everybody's home. Everybody knows everybody else. And you don't let anything get in the way of having a great time.

Pretty soon, Carla and Gabrielle, two girls from school, bring me down to the waterfront. There are a bunch of kids wading in the river, some of them up to their knees. Believe it or not, my dad already anticipated this. As soon as he heard Ronnie's address, he went into a lecture about how I was not to dip any body part into the mighty St. Clair.

"You can freeze your butt off in the water" were his exact words. "You can also lower your resistance and get sick again. Don't be an idiot."

The girls kick off their shoes and start splashing

around, but I hang back. For some reason, I can't help thinking about something else ZeeBee told me about Centerlight's gangster past: When there were too many government agents watching the town, the rumrunners would deliver their shipments via the river to private beaches. They used those flat-bottomed Higgins boats—the ones that would become legendary as landing craft on D-Day during World War Two. I could never quite picture it before, but this would be the perfect place for it. For all I know, Tommy-Gun Ferguson once stood on this very spot, watching his guys unload crates of illegal booze from Canada.

The thought of ZeeBee sours my mood a little. Practically every kid in town our age must be here, but not her. A lot of what she says may be pure baloney, but her complaints about being left out are 100 percent real.

I feel a twinge of guilt. I actually considered asking Ronnie if I could bring ZeeBee along tonight. What better way to reintroduce her to the kids who should have been her friends all along? But in the end, I wimped out. I just got to Centerlight. Who am I to issue invitations to Ronnie's party-that-isn't-a-party? I'm probably on the thin ice of the guest list myself.

I shake my head to clear it. Even though ZeeBee

isn't with me tonight, she's here just the same—on this beach and in the hole Barney made in the fence. In a weird way, she's like tuberculosis. Even when she's not physically present, her influence is still around.

A faint spray strikes me full in the face. Carla and Gabrielle are splashing and waving.

"Get over here, Keenan!" Carla orders. "Water's great!"

I kick off my shoes and roll up my jeans. Sorry, Dad. It's not that I didn't get your message. I'm just choosing to ignore it.

The water is chilly, although not as cold as I expect. Even at ankle depth I can feel the river current. Farther out, a boy who's in up to his chest suddenly disappears. I'm terrified he's a goner and his corpse will wash up downstream in Detroit. But a few seconds later, his friends yank him to the surface and haul him ashore, choking and sputtering. Everybody's laughing and cheering, even the almost-victim, who's punching the air in celebration between coughs.

Got it. Near-death experiences are just part of the fun.

Carla and Gabrielle wade farther to join some guys who are playing monkey-in-the-middle with a football. I retreat to the shore and kick back into my shoes.

The sun is all the way down now. The temperature is dropping, and the last thing I need is to get drenched. See, Dad? I'm not being an idiot.

I retrace my steps to the warmth of the firepit, which seems to be the center of things.

"En garde!" barks a voice, and a flaming wooden stick whizzes past my face, missing my nose by about half an inch. What is it with these kids and swordplay?

His opponent parries the blow with a hot dog bun, which instantly breaks in half. Stick and bread hit the grass, both burning. I stub out the fire with the toe of my sneaker, since neither combatant bothers to. Either that or they're both laughing too hard to notice.

I catch a glimpse of a dark-haired woman peering nervously out a second-story window at the mayhem below. Mrs. Lindahl, I conclude. Ronnie's right; she doesn't like confrontation. She'd rather risk setting her property on fire than tell her son something he doesn't want to hear. Our eyes meet, and she quickly turns away, shutting the curtain behind her.

Now that it's fully dark, the yard has gotten a lot more crowded. We're almost belly-to-belly, so in order to move around, you kind of have to part the sea of people in front of you. I don't recognize a lot of the new faces. I get the feeling that they're older—eighth graders, or maybe even kids from the high school.

The patio serves as the dance floor, if you can call it that. There's more jumping than dancing going on. The music is cranked up pretty loud. You can feel the pounding of the bass in your belly.

The door to the Lindahls' garden shed is open, and there are kids play-fighting with hoes and rakes. Someone has torn into a fifty-pound bag of grass seed, and there's a full-fledged battle going on, as handfuls are flung in all directions. I catch a face-full, which starts me coughing and spitting. It scares the daylights out of me—I've spent the whole summer trying to *stop* coughing. I'm not anxious to go back to the bad old days.

As I stagger around in search of breathing space, I'm nearly plowed down by a wheelbarrow pushed by a burly eighth grader. Riding in the payload are Carla and Gabrielle, both soaked to the skin and coated with grass seed. I dive out of the way and the barrow smacks full force into the fence, dumping the girls onto the grass. The fence holds strong, which makes me wonder how hard Barney must have hit it to blast right through.

Lying on the grass, I catch a glimpse of Ronnie. He hasn't entirely lost his host-with-the-most grin, but it's starting to sag around the edges. He's standing with a couple of adults—probably neighbors—who are shouting at him, not out of anger, but because there's no other way to be heard over the roar in the backyard. I catch a word here and there: "Too crowded . . ." "Noise complaint . . ." And "Calling the cops . . ."

I get the picture. Maybe Ronnie's mother wants to pretend that the P-word isn't happening tonight. But if the police get involved, it's hard to imagine that the news won't find its way to his father.

Ronnie disappears into the crowd and, a few minutes later, the music dies suddenly. Over the rising cry of outrage, Ronnie is calling, "Come on, you guys! We've got to quiet down . . ."

A chorus of boos greets this announcement. People throw grass seed, marshmallows, soda, and the occasional hot dog in Ronnie's direction.

The music comes back on at half volume, but the gathering is never the same. The dancers disperse, and the crowd thins out, most of them exiting through the Barney hole in the fence. The complaining neighbors leave too, still miffed, but satisfied that order has been restored.

I don't think Ronnie is ready for the condition of his lawn now that we can see it again. It looks like someone ran a cattle drive through here. Mashed hot dogs, buns, marshmallows, and potato chips are strewn to the four winds. Grass seed is everywhere, but that might be a good thing. The lawn is so torn up that planting a new one can't be a bad idea.

Joey runs onto the scene, a toilet seat around his neck like a garland of flowers. "Ronnie, man, what happened? Where's everybody going?"

"My buzz-kill neighbors threatened to call the cops on us," Ronnie gripes. "They made me turn down the music."

"So? Let's take it into the basement," Joey persists. "Plenty of room down there."

Ronnie seems to consider this for a moment. Then he takes a long look at the wreckage of the yard. "Forget it," he says finally. "Let's get out of here. This place is boring."

That's how I end up joining the migration of kids straggling into the road in front of Ronnie's house. A lot of them are climbing onto bikes that lean against the fence the full length of the Lindahl property. I take out my phone and start dialing home for Dad to come pick me up.

"Hey, Keenan," comes a voice. "What are you doing?"

It's Carla, perched on a mountain bike.

"Calling for a ride."

"Come with us!" she interrupts.

"I don't have my bike—" Actually, it's Wayne Tice's bike, not mine. But this doesn't seem like the time and place to explain that.

In answer, she grabs me by the shirt and hauls me onto the seat behind her. It's soaking wet from Carla's dip in the river.

"Uh—are you sure this is safe?" I stammer.

"What are you—five?"

She gestures around us with a sweep of her hand. It looks like the starting line of the Tour de France, with kids riding double and even triple on bikes in bold defiance of the Michigan cops and their rules.

The challenge is clear: Nobody else has a problem with this. What am I afraid of?

For starters, I'm afraid of being thrown off a speeding bicycle in the pitch dark. I'm afraid of winding up with a concussion before I'm fully recovered from my last serious health issue. But here, surrounded by my entire grade, this seems like the manhood test I have to pass. I stay put on the back of the seat.

There are a few garbled arguments about what the plan is. Then we all pedal off—in different directions.

I hang on to Carla for dear life, positive that if I loosen my grip for even a split second, I'll be pitched overboard into the ditch. As we ride, the wind blows the grass seed from Carla's damp clothes into me. It's all I can do to stave off another coughing fit. If there's a Wikipedia page on how *not* to recover from tuberculosis, I'm pretty sure I'm nailing it tonight.

At first it seems as if we're just cycling randomly around the western shore. Every now and then, we spot another bike from the party, and the other riders yell insults at us and laugh their heads off.

"Where are we going?" I call up to Carla.

"I'm just following everybody else," she shouts back.

"But no one's following *any*body else!" I protest.

I can feel my phone vibrating in my pocket. Probably Dad, wondering where I am. I'd answer it, but I honestly have no idea what to tell him. We're in the woods now, and bikes are joining us from all directions, forming a convoy. Soon, the pavement ends, and we're jouncing along what must be a dirt road.

And then a sudden super-bright light flashes above us. That's when I realize that I *know* this place. We're on our way to the lighthouse!

A few minutes later, our caravan of bikes pulls up to the base of the old stone structure. I jump down, savoring the feeling of solid ground under my feet.

Joey seems amazed to see me and pulls me into a bear hug. "Keenan! You came!"

Ronnie slaps me on the shoulder. "You're a good dude, sweetie."

As if being dragged along by a crazy girl counts as an act of loyalty.

The lighthouse is locked, but Ronnie opens it by sliding his student ID card between the door and the jamb. There's a roar of approval and we all tromp inside the small building.

Kids rush up the metal staircase and, a moment later, come sliding down the spiral bannister, whooping and cheering. As we climb, a few lunatics reenact WWE wrestling moves on the steps, where one false move could wipe out a dozen of us. The place is as bright as high noon every time the big light flashes on, and pitch-black when it winks out. The chorus of "Ooh!" followed by "Aah!" is making me seasick. Queasy, I peer down over the railing at a surprisingly orderly line of people waiting their turn to use the Canadian bathroom.

Eventually, everybody ends up in the watch room, one level below the light. A few kids venture up the ladder to the top to project giant shadow puppets on the shores of Michigan and Ontario. But the big lantern is so powerful that they come down fast, blinking and dazed. My phone vibrates again. Dad; now it's official. This time I don't answer because I know exactly where I am, and I'm not supposed to be here. None of us are.

The idea of breaking into a lighthouse might have seemed cool, but seventeen of us packed into the watch room can't find much to do. Pretty soon, the WWE crew revives the smackdown from the stairs. Before anyone can stop it, an errant elbow catches Joey in the side of the head. He stumbles backward into the computer table and lands, butt-first, on the keyboard. The big light winks out abruptly.

We hold our breath, waiting for the next flash, counting silently: *One Mississippi . . . two Mississippi . . .*

Nothing happens.

"Dude!" Ronnie accuses. "You busted the lighthouse!"

"It's not my fault!" Joey defends himself in the darkness. "DeVonte pushed me!"

"Yeah," DeVonte mutters, "well it's not my fault that double-wide caboose of yours hit the wrong button!"

Phones appear and flashlight beams fix on the computer. A few of the eighth graders lean over the screen, searching for a way to undo the damage. Somebody Facetimes a kid named Ziggy, who seems to be the school's tech whiz. But while Ziggy may be a genius at computers, he doesn't know anything about lighthouses. He doesn't recognize any of the error messages that are coming thick and fast.

I step forward. "Mind if I take a crack at it?"

The eighth graders stare at me. "Who are you?"

"That's Keenan," Carla supplies. "He can fix it. He lived in Lesotho!"

I can hardly believe nobody questions that. But the truth is, I have an idea of how I might be able to get the beacon going again. It has nothing to do with the places I've lived and everything to do with ZeeBee's dad—what he did that time the Geek Squad was stuck on the bridge to mainland Michigan.

In the cone of light from several phones, I get down on my hands and knees, pull out the power cord, count to five, then plug it back in again and turn the computer on. It begins to reboot.

For a couple of minutes, all eyes are on the glowing screen. The silence is so total that we can almost hear the collective pounding of our hearts.

And then the beacon emits its brilliant flash, lighting up the room.

I get mobbed by every one of them—hugged, pounded, high-fived. Carla even plants a kiss on my cheek. It's a true celebration, and even though I didn't really do much, it feels good to be the hero of the hour. There's a rush up the ladder. Now that we've got the light back, people want to bathe in it.

The euphoria doesn't last long. "Guys," comes a voice from upstairs. "Company's coming."

I scramble up the ladder just high enough to be able to see out the window. They're right! Centerlight is sleepy and quiet, but a single car makes its way through the town toward us, a flasher on the roof. Cops.

"Let's get out of here!" Ronnie bawls.

No words were ever less necessary. The stampede has already started.

I'm climbing down to the watch room when a big boot from above stomps on my hand. With a cry of pain, I lose my balance and land flat on my back on the wood floor. Stunned, I lie there while the place empties.

Outside, I can hear anxious voices and bicycle tires crunching on gravel. "Wait for me!" I howl, throwing myself at the spiral staircase. I run down and around, down and around, but by the time I reach the bottom and scramble into the night, there isn't a bike in sight. I'm stranded, all alone.

No—not alone. In the distance, up the dirt road, a pair of headlights is coming my way. The flashers whirl above them.

The police!

9

Border Officer Darryl Tice

'm a Centrelight guy, born and bred, and it's fair to say I love the place. Where else can you watch the sun rise over Ontario and set over Michigan, all in a place where two nations get along just fine? Oh sure, we'll squabble over small matters, like whose coins are jamming up the vending machines—the American ones; the quarters are too fat. But for the most part, both countries know how lucky they are to have each other as neighbors.

I brought my wife here from Calgary twenty years ago, and if she hates it, she hasn't mentioned it yet. We've raised two kids here, and I have to admit that's gotten trickier. In my day, they had a Canadian school on the island, but it closed up years ago, as our side of the island turned into more of a retirement community. Today, the kids take a ferry to the school in Corunna. My son, Wayne, didn't mind so much. He had a tight-knit group of friends, and complaining about the boat ride was a uniting factor for them. I worry about my daughter, ZeeBee, though. By sheer bad luck, she's the only one in her age group on the Canadian side. And she hasn't been able to bond with the Americans here or with the Canadians she goes to school with on the mainland.

It's hard on the girl, and not so easy on the wife and me either. When ZeeBee's not happy, no one else is allowed to be happy. Over the summer, she made friends with this American kid who was laid up with tuberculosis. But she's afraid that, now that he's started school with the locals, he'll forget all about her. Her mother and I try to be reassuring. It won't happen, we tell her. It's like talking to the wall. Once our Zarabeth makes her mind up about something, that's pretty much it.

Aside from that worry, we've got a pretty nice life here. I have a lot of seniority with Canada Border Services, which is interesting work I enjoy. The job would be paradise—if it weren't for that stupid lighthouse.

Don't get me wrong. It's a national treasure—for two nations, really. But when something goes wrong, why does it always have to be on Canada's day?

That's why I'm heading down the dirt road at quarter to eleven on a Saturday night. The beacon conked out. If only it could have waited till midnight, it would have been the Americans' problem. And guess who's standing guard for the True North, Strong and Free? Officer Darryl Tice, patsy.

The worst part is, as I'm driving, I can see that everything's fine and the light is back on again. But it's still my job to see what went wrong—like I don't already know. A bunch of yahoos, teenagers most likely. When they can't think of anything to do, sooner or later, the locked door of the lighthouse proves irresistible.

As I jounce along the dirt road, a fleet of bicycles flashes through my headlights, pedaling frantically back to town. Wow, the troublemakers are getting younger every year. I expected high school kids, but this lot doesn't seem any older than ZeeBee!

I make no move to stop anybody. What would be the point? We'd just hand them over to their parents anyway. It would make my Saturday night that much longer.

By the time I get near the lighthouse, the bikes are long gone, so I assume the drama is all over.

No such luck.

As I pull up to the door, the figure of a boy dashes out of the lighthouse, stops cold when he sees me, hesitates an instant, and takes off into the woods.

I jump to the ground. "Come back, kid! It's okay!"

Apparently, he doesn't think so. He keeps on running.

"Aw, no!" I start after him. What choice do I have? He'll trip on a root and knock himself silly on a rock or something.

As I gallop along in hot pursuit, I take a flashlight from my belt and aim the beam at the fleeing figure. Part of this is so I don't lose sight of him, but mostly it's to make sure *I'm* not the one who ends up unconscious on the forest floor. Meanwhile, the lighthouse keeps giving us its blazing roundabout, making it even harder to concentrate on where I'm going.

Who do I think I'm kidding—a man my age trying to run down a middle schooler? He's going to be fine while I stroke out eating his dust.

No sooner has the thought crossed my mind than it happens. Out of nowhere, the kid slows down, stumbling in the underbrush like he's forgotten how to put one foot in front of the other. A few seconds later, he's lying flat on his face in the dirt.

I try to yell, "Are you okay?" but who's got the breath? I'm not annoyed anymore. I'm just worried that the kid's really hurt. In a burst of speed I didn't know I had left, I race up to the boy, kneel beside him, and roll him over onto his back.

"Speak to me, kid!"

He's even shorter of breath than I am. His eyelids flutter open and he regards me in horror.

Oh boy. I recognize him. It's ZeeBee's friend—Keenan.

10

Zarabeth

Of course I'm mad. Wouldn't you be? I warned Keenan that Ronnie and those jerks are bad news. Well, maybe *warned* is too strong a word. But I definitely told him that they're jerks. And what did he do with the information? He got himself invited to a party! Not just any party—going by the evidence, it was the middle school blowout of the year.

Oh yeah, I know all about that. After Dad found Keenan passed out in the woods by the lighthouse, he did a little detective work. Keenan didn't rat anybody out (he's being loyal to his new buddies, even if he has zero loyalty to the person who stayed by his side when he was too sick to leave his own backyard). But Dad wouldn't be much of a border officer if he didn't have the brains to reconstruct a crime scene. He passed every single one of those boneheads as they biked away from the lighthouse. Plus the inside was littered with chip bags, gum wrappers, and pop cans.

I may be the big outsider, but I know what that means. One of those nitwits had a wild party, and when the noise complaints shut it down, they moved the festivities to the most obvious public space on the island.

"You're right on the money," Dad tells me at breakfast the next morning. "I called over to the police station last night. The Americans confirm some complaints about an address on Shore Drive—the Lindahl house."

Ronnie! Why am I not surprised? "Yeah, but what made you go out to the lighthouse in the first place? There couldn't be noise complaints there. It's in the middle of nowhere."

He shrugs. "The light went out. It was Saturday night, so the call went to me. A couple of hours later and your friend would have been at the mercy of the Geek Squad." He frowns. "Funny thing, though. When I got there, the beacon was working fine."

"False alarm?" I ask.

He shakes his head. "Keenan wouldn't say a word, but I think I know what happened. Those partying dummies messed up the computer, and Keenan remembered what I did that day. It's not rocket science; it's just a reboot." He chuckles. "Sharp kid."

"Sharp?" I echo in outrage. "Keenan Cardinal is a complete idiot!"

Mum looks up. "Don't speak ill of people until you've walked a mile in their shoes."

"Keenan couldn't walk a mile in his own shoes until I nursed him back to health," I say bitterly.

"Don't exaggerate," my mother interrupts. "You befriended him at a difficult time, and that was very nice of you. But you aren't exactly Florence Nightingale."

On the floor at my feet, Barney Two sits up and begs for the piece of bacon on my fork. I eat it without offering it to him. The real Barney would have been up on the table, helping himself to the entire dish.

"You're defending him," I accuse. "This juvenile delinquent who vandalizes *our* lighthouse—"

"Only because it was Saturday," Mum points out.

"—dragging Dad out of bed in the middle of the night to go and arrest him."

"I didn't arrest him," Dad says wearily. "I took him home to his father and explained the whole thing. The poor kid was exhausted and scared to death—it's not so long ago that he was really sick."

"But you're pressing charges, right?" I persist. "I mean, Canada is?"

"Brad Cardinal promised to bring in a cleaning crew to sweep out the lighthouse," Dad informs me. "That's all Canada expects from your pal Keenan. We want to put it behind us so we can go back to thinking about Drake and who's going to win the Stanley Cup."

"Keenan Cardinal is not my pal. I'm *done* with that guy!"

"Because he was mixed up in a little trouble at the lighthouse?" Mum asks in surprise. "What's gotten into you, ZeeBee? You two are friends."

"We *were* friends," I amend. "But the minute he started at that school, I got dropped like a hot potato because he got a better offer. I don't get invited to the kind of parties where you disturb the peace and trash lighthouses."

They don't say any more. They know me almost better than I know myself.

Keenan doesn't call to apologize. He doesn't text either.

My parents shrug it off.

"His cell is probably on an American plan," Mum reasons.

"Or a Chinese plan," I muse.

She's triumphant. "I'm sure it's something like that."

That still doesn't explain why he doesn't come over to say he's sorry in person—which won't work, by the way. I've already decided to freeze him out.

So where is he?

I run into Ronnie at Mr. Chaiken's market and growl, "Tell your friend Keenan thanks for disappearing off the face of the earth. You know, my dad had to play paramedic after you guys marooned him at the lighthouse on Saturday. He didn't even have the courtesy to come by our house to thank him."

"That's not it," Ronnie replies seriously. "Keenan's grounded. His dad went ape when he found out what happened."

"How come *you're* not grounded?" I ask. "I'll bet you trashed your whole house."

"Just the backyard." His eyes shine with memory.

Well, that makes me feel better, but not much. Keenan hasn't come by because he's not allowed out. But that doesn't mean he wouldn't be ignoring me anyway—the way he ignores everybody who isn't on the A-list party circuit.

Anyway, just because he's grounded doesn't mean I can't give him a piece of my mind. I found him when he was laid up with TB, and I can find him now.

When I head over to his house, Barney Two following me like a bad smell, I half expect to find Keenan on the lawn chair in the backyard like before. But this time I have to go ring the bell.

When he finally answers the door, he looks so over-joyed to see me that I'm almost glad to see him too.

"Hiya, Barney Two!" He drops to his knees, rolls the little dog over, and rubs his furry stomach enthusiastically.

It bugs me. "I'm here too, or has the TB morphed into a weird vision thing where you can't see Canadians? Passing out near a lighthouse does strange things to people."

At the icy sarcasm in my voice, Barney Two twists away from Keenan and pops back upright, looking abashed.

Keenan gets to his feet. "Hi, ZeeBee," he says sheepishly. "Come on in."

I step inside, Barney Two slipping in behind me. I'm secretly rooting for the dog to make a mess in the living room. That would be a more perfect statement of what I'm feeling than anything I could put into words. But I know he won't. He's too well behaved. If it was the real Barney, Keenan's father would have to throw away this house and get a new one.

"Good news," I tell Keenan. "My dad convinced Canada to drop the charges against you."

He turns pale. "Charges?"

"You know, breaking and entering, trashing a historic landmark, face-planting in a public forest, being too stupid to listen to advice."

Keenan's famous brow arches. "What advice?"

"I told you about Ronnie and those idiots. And what did you go and do? Become best buddies with them."

He looks mystified. "You told me you and Ronnie didn't get along. What does that have to do with me?"

"They stranded you out there, didn't they?" I challenge. "Your 'friends' took off and left you to face the rap."

"It wasn't like that," he says earnestly. "There was

a rush to get out of the lighthouse when we spotted someone coming. I slipped on the ladder, and by the time I made it through the door, everybody was gone."

"And when you were running from my dad like a common criminal, did you have a chance to think that *I* wouldn't have done that to you?" I persist.

He's still confused. "How could you do anything? You weren't there. You weren't even invited to—" Sudden understanding. "Is that what this is about? That I got invited to Ronnie's and you didn't?"

I don't answer. I stare at him intently. They say that Tommy-Gun Ferguson had a look like this—right before he iced you.

"ZeeBee, come on," he argues. "I was going to see if you could come with me, but I didn't know how welcome I'd be myself. I've only just met these kids. I promise I'll ask about you if I ever get invited to anything else."

I'm ticked off already, but that really puts me over the top. "I don't need your help with my social life, thanks very much!" And I wheel away from him.

"ZeeBee, wait—" he pleads.

Too late. I storm out of the house and start down the

walk, turning only when I hear the door open again behind me. "This better be good!" I blare.

"You forgot your dog," he says apologetically.

Barney Two comes bounding up, his liquid eyes full of devotion. It makes me even madder. On the other hand, at least he's choosing me over Keenan, which shows a certain amount of good judgment. That's more than I can say for the kids on this island.

I'm still fuming when I cross back into Canada and start up the street to our house. I decide to enter through the back door. If I go in the front, my mother will see how upset I am. That's not a conversation I'm in the mood to have.

I slip in through the side gate, and I'm almost at the back when I freeze in front of a small flowerbed up against the foundation. There, in the flattened earth, are two boot prints.

My eyes narrow. That flowerbed is directly in front of the narrow window that opens into our basement. Someone stood there and spied into our house!

My heartbeat ramps up a little. I've heard voices in the night, footsteps, the opening and closing of car doors. Once, I'm pretty sure I even saw a flashlight beam in our backyard. Mum and Dad always convinced me that I'm overdramatic, and I must be dreaming. But this is hard physical evidence. This time nobody can say I'm imagining things.

I run into the house. "Dad! Come quick! You've got to see this!"

He's upstairs, listening to ship transmissions on the St. Clair River. He does that before going on duty. I drag him out to the flowerbed.

"You're not going to tell me I dreamed this!" I exclaim triumphantly.

He shrugs. "I have a pair of boots with treads like that."

"And did you stand right there, staring into the basement?" I demand.

"No, but I turned over the earth in that flowerbed. Who remembers how my feet were set when I stopped to blow my nose? You know my allergies."

I can't win. It's all Barney Two's fault. If the real Barney was still around, we wouldn't be arguing over boot prints. We'd be getting their owner down from the tree he climbed to avoid being chomped to death.

So I drop it. But when Dad goes to work, I find those boots he's talking about and take them out to the flowerbed. He's right—the treads are a perfect match.

Frowning, I take the pair and place them inside the impressions in the earth.

Maybe it's just me, but those prints look like they were made by boots that are a little bigger than my father's.

11

Keenan

My fist makes a loud slapping sound as it slams into the kickboxing pad.

"Anyway, the good news is my tuberculosis didn't come back," I say, panting a little.

"Keep working!" Bryce orders. "No excuses!"

I hit it again. *Wham!*

"Combo!" he barks.

Both fists. *Wham! Wham!*

"Doing fine," he reports.

"Last week I was doing amazing," I remind him.

He shrugs. "A little setback. So what?"

"Little setback," I repeat. "Have you ever fainted? Your whole life stops and you're waking up in the middle of it."

"Once." The trainer blocks another blow. "After my first triathlon. I didn't hydrate properly."

I grin. "No excuses."

"Smart guy," he snorts. "Kick!"

I raise my knee and snap my lower leg into the pad. Not bad!

"Again!"

With a rush of misplaced confidence, I aim my foot at a spot at the center of Bryce's chest. Luckily, Bryce sees it coming. He drops the pads and gets his arms under me before I land on my head.

"There's a gap between what we *think* we can do and what we really can," he lectures. "With me, it's making French toast without burning it."

"I really thought I could land it this time," I pant.

"And you will," he promises, "when you're ready. And on that day, I'll have you over for the best French toast you've ever tasted."

I can't quite explain it, but landing that kick would prove that I'm still the old me. Who knows? It might even mean that it's time for me to go back to Mom, Klaus, and my friends in Shanghai.

"We're running late today," Bryce says. "Here's my four o'clock." He introduces me to a middle-aged man with a shaved head and a neat beard and mustache. "Peter Tolenski, meet Keenan Cardinal. He's the kid I was telling you about."

"Don't believe him about the French toast," Mr. Tolenski advises me. "Pure motivational drivel."

"Peter rents a house on the Canadian side," Bryce explains. "He's been working on a book about Centerlight's history during Prohibition."

"Cool," I say without much enthusiasm. The topic makes me think of ZeeBee and puts a bad taste in my mouth. I know she's mad about Saturday, but she really, truly seems to hate me now. She doesn't answer calls or texts, and I can't keep sending them forever because it's so expensive. My emails get ignored. And I can't go find her, because I'm still grounded for another week. I'm down to two destinations: school and the gym.

"You're the boy with the tae kwon do kick," the writer concludes.

"So far, I'm the boy with*out* the tae kwon do kick," I correct him ruefully.

Mr. Tolenski gestures toward Bryce. "I've experienced his French toast," he confides to me. "Overrated."

"Keep talking, old man," Bryce warns. "I'll have you doing squat-thrusts all afternoon."

It's like a comedy routine as they go back and forth at each other. I'm smiling as I step out of Island Fitness.

The bellow comes at top volume, shouted from about three inches behind my left ear. "Boo!"

I practically hit the moon. And when I come back down again, Ronnie and Joey are standing on the sidewalk, grinning at me with pride, as if they've just accomplished something wonderful.

"Real mature, you guys!"

"*Mature*," Joey muses, brow furrowed. "Don't think I know that word. We need to study it in vocabulary."

"What you really need is to stop jumping out at people and giving them heart attacks."

"That too," Ronnie agrees amiably. "Hey, thought you were grounded, sweetie. What are you doing in town?"

"Gym," I reply. "Besides school, it's the one place I'm allowed to go."

Joey nods. "We know. We were waiting for you."

"For what?"

"Follow us," Ronnie orders.

"I can't. I just said I have to go home."

"You *are* going home," he argues. "This is on the way—sort of. You're taking the long way home."

"Check this out." Joey reaches into his pocket and produces a small floppy red plastic item.

"A balloon?" I ask dubiously.

Joey steps up to a drinking fountain and folds the balloon's opening over the spout. The red plastic swells as it fills up with water.

"A beautiful thing," Ronnie approves.

I'm genuinely interested. "What's it for?"

"Not what," Joey says, tying the balloon closed. "*Who.* I say we climb up on the roof of the hairdresser's and drop it on the fanciest, poofiest head that comes out."

"Nah," Ronnie scoffs. "Let's take it to the river and chuck it at a speedboat. We'll get better impact if the target's moving fast."

"Nuh-uh." Joey holds the water bomb away from him. "My balloon, my rules."

Ronnie reaches for it. "But it'll be *better*—"

As the two grapple for the balloon, they fumble it up into the air. It comes down between the three of us and vaporizes as it hits the pavement, drenching us from the knees down. There's a split second of shocked silence and then the two of them dissolve into laughter.

"Very funny, you guys," I snarl. "Now how am I going to explain that I went straight home from the gym? My dad'll think I waded along the shore."

That only makes them laugh harder. They stumble to a bench and collapse onto it. That does it for me. It's impossible to stay serious when two failed water-bombers are losing their minds in front of you. I crack up too.

The mournful horn of the ferry from Corunna sounds in the distance. It sobers me instantly. I picture ZeeBee trudging onto the dock, complaining about the late boat due to mist on the river, or choppy water, or whatever. For ZeeBee, the specifics aren't important. What matters is the complaining.

These days, her biggest complaint is me. It's not fair. What have I ever done to her except be her friend? What is she so mad at me for? Is it because her dad had to peel me off the grass and haul me home? She knows I wasn't the only one at the lighthouse that night.

As that thought passes through my brain, I realize that the question is the answer. I *wasn't* alone that night, just like I'm not alone right now. Even though I'm new on Centerlight, I'm the one who gets invited to stuff. I'm the one with friends to sit on a bench and laugh with. And by some random quirk of borders and where she goes to school, ZeeBee isn't. She always ends up on the outside looking in.

It's not my fault. I haven't done anything wrong. It's just the way things are. But that makes it even worse, because there's nothing I can do to fix it.

Ronnie and Joey are still cackling when a big black Mercedes squeals up to the curb and out jumps a burly middle-aged man with a buzz cut and the kind of sunglasses Secret Service guys wear.

Ronnie leaps up as if he's been burned. "My dad! Hide the water balloon!"

The "balloon" is currently a shredded piece of plastic no larger than a wad of chewing gum, but Joey still manages to kick it under the bench to hide the evidence. Apparently, Mr. Lindahl is someone you don't mess with.

Ronnie's father is short and stocky, yet his clothes hang on him like they've been made to measure. He wears those special golf shoes with the leather fringe that hangs over the laces. It flops as he marches over.

"You promised Mom you'd sweep out the garage

today. What are you doing here?"

"I'll do it now." Ronnie starts for the car, then turns to introduce me. "Dad, this is that new kid, Keenan."

Mr. Lindahl gives me a quick once-over with his eyes, but doesn't bother to say hello, goodbye, or drop dead. "Let's go," he urges his son.

With an embarrassed look at Joey and me, Ronnie gets into the Mercedes. He's so wet that he sloshes into the glove-leather bucket seat like he's sailing down a waterslide.

The reaction from his father is explosive. *"Get out of my car!"* In a split second, his face is bright purple and his eyes are red-rimmed and bulging. He yanks Ronnie bodily out of the seat, sending him sprawling on the grass.

"You told me to get in!" Ronnie squeaks.

"If my leather is damaged," his father threatens, "it's coming out of your college account!"

Joey and I stand there, cowed. I can't speak for Joey, but I've never seen anybody blow up that high that fast.

"So how am I supposed to get home?" Ronnie asks plaintively.

And just like that, Mr. Lindahl is back to normal— not nice exactly, but no longer in a towering rage.

"You've got legs," he replies. "Use them." And he gets back in the car and roars away.

Ronnie shoots Joey and me a crooked grin. "What?" As if we haven't just witnessed his father melting down like a nuclear power plant.

Joey laughs, but I can't. It was just too awkward, bordering on scary.

My wet shoes squelch all the way home.

12

Bradley Cardinal

Keenan looks a lot like his mother, my ex-wife. They have the same fair complexion, the same blue eyes, the same medium brown hair. He's even got that eyebrow that the two of them can raise to such dramatic effect.

I definitely saw my fair share of that when Lila and I were married. I saw it again on Skype when I told her that her son would be starting seventh grade on

Centerlight, rather than going back to China. But she was good about following the doctor's recommendation. That's the one thing we agree on—we both want what's best for Keenan.

"So when does Dr. Sobel think it will be okay for him to come home?" she asks me now.

I still find it amazing to Skype her. She's sitting at a computer in her room; I'm sitting at a computer in mine. Then I remember: outside her window, that's *China*—the other side of the world.

"We have to wait for his immune system to build itself back up," I explain. "The TB is over—he's recovered from that. But look how he crashed again after that lighthouse incident. That shouldn't happen to a normal twelve-year-old."

"It wouldn't have happened if he hadn't been at the lighthouse in the first place," she reminds me.

I shrug. "The kid has to live, Lila. We can't pack him in bubble wrap just because he's been sick. The doctor wants to err on the side of caution, which means Keenan could be here for months."

And she reluctantly agrees.

"It's just hard," she confides, "to think that he's seven thousand miles away from me."

"When he's with you," I can't help reminding her, "he's seven thousand miles away from *me*."

I'd never wish tuberculosis on anybody. But I have to confess it's been nice having Keenan with me, even if it's just temporary. He was only five when his mom and I split. And within a few months of that, she got her first international school job—Brussels, I think, or was it Helsinki? I feel like I've missed most of his childhood, so I'm soaking it up now, since it isn't going to last. If that means the occasional eruption of lighthouse-mania, I'll cope. He's a great kid. I'm lucky.

I sign off with Lila just as the doorbell rings. By the time I make it downstairs, Keenan is ushering Bryce into the living room.

It was my idea to have the trainer over for dinner. The guy lives on the island all alone, so he's probably surviving on Taco Bell and protein shakes. But he's been so good for Keenan that I want to encourage the friendship. I already see the physical difference in my son. He's breathing better, moving with athletic confidence and grace, building a pair of real shoulders.

We all head out back to fire up the barbecue.

Keenan indicates the lawn chair, which is still sitting

in the center of the yard. "That used to be my whole life before I started training with you," he tells Bryce. "I spent ten hours a day in that thing, lying around like a carrot."

"Inactivity," Bryce clucks. "Not a fan. I'm a fan of that, though," he adds, as I place the steaks on the hot grill.

Funny thing about Bryce. The big man communicates mostly through a series of grunts, plus a vocabulary of about twenty words. But he launches into a detailed lecture on the nutritional properties of red meat, including the number of grams of protein per ounce, when cooked medium rare, which is the way he likes it, please.

I take in his tattoos and the nasty scar on his forearm. Tough guy. He grew up in the same Chicago neighborhood I did, and it wasn't always the kindest place. That's another reason I like his influence on Keenan, who's normally surrounded by Lila's overly sensitive teacher crowd. The kid needs to learn that the world isn't always so warm and fuzzy.

Keenan is still talking about his long weeks in the backyard. "I wasn't *allowed* to be active. Doctor's orders."

Bryce raises a hand to his ear. "Do I hear excuses?"

"Put the cuffs on me," I jump in. "If I let him relapse, his mother would have swum all the way from China to feed me through the wood-chipper."

"It wasn't so terrible," Keenan tells us. "That's how I met ZeeBee. And Barney Two."

"Weird name for a dog," Bryce comments.

"The original Barney died before I got here," Keenan goes on, "but supposedly he was pretty notorious on the island."

Bryce shrugs. "Never heard of him."

I laugh. "Then you must spend a lot of time wearing noise-canceling headphones. You didn't have to know Barney to hear him. He used to howl the island down. I'll bet he drew noise complaints in Detroit."

"Maybe even in China," Keenan adds. "But Barney Two's great. Such a good dog—smart and real loyal too!"

Bryce seems interested. "Sounds like you and this girl are pretty close."

"I guess we used to be," Keenan replies. "She kind of hates me now."

"She doesn't hate you," I put in. "She probably just feels funny because her dad had to peel you off the forest floor and arrest you."

"He didn't arrest me," he points out. "He just gave me a lift home."

"Yeah," I say with a wink at Bryce, who's taking all this in. "A lift home from juvenile delinquency, breaking and entering, and a serious health relapse—things he wouldn't let his daughter get involved in."

"Only because she wasn't invited," Keenan snaps back defensively. "As much as she complains about them, ZeeBee would jump at the chance to be a part of that crowd. That's why she's so bitter—not because she hates what they do, but because she wants to do it too."

"Don't worry," I tell Keenan. "She won't stay mad forever." I feel a little absurd dispensing this advice. Me, whose ex-wife moved all the way to China just to put some distance between us.

"I don't know, Dad. You're talking about the president of the Tommy-Gun Ferguson Fan Club. He doesn't strike me as having been the forgiving type, and ZeeBee isn't either."

"Tommy-Gun Ferguson?" Bryce repeats. "What do you think of those old stories? The gangsters? The lost gold?"

"It keeps the tourists coming." I pile the sizzling steaks onto a serving plate. "We have achieved medium rare. Somebody grab the potatoes."

And so help me, Bryce does—bare-handed off the hot grill, without so much as a peep. Those muscles must go all the way to the top of his head.

13

Keenan

'm a legend.

I know this because Ronnie says: "Dude, you're a legend."

"How do you figure that?"

"You've proven yourself a million different ways," he assures me. "You fixed a whole lighthouse like a boss. You know where Lethoso is."

"Lesotho," I correct him.

"You got interrogated by the cops and you didn't rat

out your friends," he persists.

"They didn't exactly put flaming bamboo under my fingernails to make me talk," I point out. "It wasn't even the real cops—just ZeeBee's dad."

"An agent of a foreign government."

"Have you met Officer Tice?" I demand. "He's like the nicest guy in the world."

"Once," he admits. "He was bringing over the check for our broken fence. He didn't seem that nice. Kind of crabby, if you ask me."

I roll my eyes. "Gee, I wonder why."

It couldn't have been fun for ZeeBee's dad to have to pay for the damage Barney did all over the island. But that's not the only reason he was probably on edge at the Lindahl house. Most of what he knows about the island kids comes from his daughter. And it's hard to imagine ZeeBee giving Ronnie a very good report.

Ronnie's right about one thing, though. Ever since my grounding ended, I'm a pretty popular guy. I'm a regular after school in Jefferson/Laurier Park. I meet Ronnie and Joey at McDonald's, Taco Bell, and the frozen yogurt place. We go to each other's houses and do homework together. Joey's convinced that Carla has a crush on me. But the more time I spend with my new friends, the more I wonder what ZeeBee is up to. It makes no sense. It's not like I kicked her out of my life. It's the opposite of that. She kicked me out of hers.

Maybe it's because she was the first person who showed me around the island. Everywhere I look now I see something she introduced me to and remember what she said about it. The dock where Capone dumped his own liquor shipment rather than hand it over to the feds. The bend in the road where Eliot Ness's car broke down and he couldn't get it fixed because Tommy-Gun threatened every mechanic on Centerlight; the cracking foundation of the old bank, which no one wants to repair because they're afraid of who they might find encased in the concrete. I don't even care that she's making most of it up—or at least inventing a lot of juicy details to add to a few bare facts. I picture the sparkle in her eye as she tells these stories, Barney Two scrambling worshipfully at her heels while she ignores him.

At first I tell myself it's just her dog that I miss—and that part's definitely true. But no, it's her too. Ronnie says she's crazy, but I think she's actually interesting. Compared to ZeeBee, the kids at my school seem pretty blah no matter how many lighthouses they break into.

I'm seeing all these places because I've been biking more and more. Bryce's idea—he wants me to up my cardio now that my wind is coming back. The thing is, it's *Wayne*'s bike, not mine. So I'm being a little fanatical about it, since one of these days ZeeBee is bound to demand I return it.

A couple of times I almost do. I get so close to ZeeBee's that I can see the cupola sticking up over the other rooftops. I always imagine the muzzle of a machine gun sticking out of it, as good old Tommy-Gun keeps his eyes peeled for enemies. More evidence of Zarabeth on the brain.

Here on the Canadian side, the houses are farther apart. As you move away from downtown, the neighborhoods thin out and give way to woods that extend to the eastern shore. I spy a footpath in among the trees, and I'm surprised ZeeBee never took me on it. On second thought, it makes perfect sense. The ZeeBee guided tour is usually about gangsters. I can't picture Bugsy Siegel spending his time wandering along some dusty trail, communing with nature and listening to the crickets.

I lean my bike against a tree and start down the path. Something about this place makes me uneasy, although I can't quite put my finger on it. Maybe it just reminds me of the woods around the lighthouse. And let's face it, that isn't a very happy memory.

I walk into a clearing and stop in my tracks. The usual assortment of forest wildlife is there—squirrels, chipmunks, birds, field mice—and it takes an instant for me to register that something's wrong. As I approach, they should be running away. But they're not moving. A wave of nausea washes over me and I stagger back a half step. They're *dead*—every single one.

It's a heartbreaking sight. There must be twenty-five or thirty of them—all small animals. This is a graveyard. It doesn't make sense. I'm no zoologist, but I know that animals don't gather in groups to kick the bucket. Why did it happen here?

I look more closely. Some of them must have died a long time ago. Their bodies are all dried up, nothing left except a little fur or a few feathers. But some of the corpses are more recent—I keep expecting them to roll over and scurry away. There are even a couple of garter snakes and what looks like a kind of miniature weasel.

The weasel's body seems to be in the best condition. Did it kill all the other animals before dying itself? No, that can't be. There would be signs of fighting—wounds on the bodies, bloodstains on the fur and skin.

I frown. There's something in the weasel's mouth, a flat gray object, encrusted with dirt and grass. I squat down to examine it. It's *food*—at least the weasel thought it was. I spot a larger piece a few feet away. It's gray, and it's obviously been nibbled at countless times, probably by these poor dead animals. That must be what killed them—they tried to eat a poisonous mushroom or something.

Only—don't animals know what plants and mushrooms to stay away from in nature? I take a closer look at the flat gray mess. That's no mushroom! I poke it with a twig. It's dried up and gross but—it's *meat*! Not meat torn from a carcass. The shape is too smooth, too regular. It's been cut by a knife, like a piece of steak or a pork chop from a butcher or supermarket.

The two ideas—*meat* and *poison*—orbit each other in my head for a few seconds before I finally put them together: *poisoned meat*. And meat doesn't just suddenly turn lethal. If there's poison in it, somebody had to put it there.

What kind of horrible person deliberately poisons a whole forest full of small animals? And for what purpose? Chipmunks, squirrels, mice, little birds, and snakes! Why would anybody do that?

When the answer comes to me, the shock is so great that my knees fold under me and I sit down cross-legged on the ground. Nobody bothers to harm a random assortment of woodland creatures. But there was one animal on Centerlight that a lot of people had a grudge against. ZeeBee must have said it fifty times: Barney was murdered. Nobody believed her because Barney was really old and because, let's face it, ZeeBee says a lot of things that are hard to believe.

But if you wanted to kill a dog and have it look like natural causes, what would the murder weapon be? A poisoned steak. And once the dog was out of the picture, the smell of meat would have been irresistible to small animals nearby.

ZeeBee Tice spins a lot of far-fetched stories about Centerlight's gangster past and even implies some pretty crazy stuff about criminals lurking around now. I don't blame the local kids for thinking she has an overactive imagination. But she didn't imagine this.

Her dog really was murdered.

14

Zarabeth

Chloe McFarlane stands on the Corunna side of the St. Clair River, pointing to different examples of sedimentary rock. I guess she knows what she's talking about. I should care more, I suppose, because I'm being graded on this too. But Chloe's in charge of the science side of our project. I'm handling cinematography—which means I'm standing in a field, filming her on my phone. That's the assignment—to produce a video about rock formations. You know, so we can post it to YouTube and get three views. Let's face it, it's pretty boring stuff. I'm having trouble paying attention, and I'm the person shooting it.

During the slow parts (in other words, all of it), I keep checking to see how many times Keenan has tried to call me. Eleven—and that's just since yesterday. Obviously, he's got something to say and he really thinks I want to hear it, since those calls cost two bucks a minute.

Well, forget it. When I make up my mind about somebody, I never change it. I don't have to, because I'm always right. I've had it with Keenan Cardinal.

"ZeeBee . . ." Chloe interrupts my reverie. "Zee-Bee!"

"Great stuff," I approve. "Really . . . geological."

"Your phone wasn't even pointed at me," my partner complains. "Now we have to start all over again."

That's Keenan's fault too, for calling a million times. It's harassment. I should get a restraining order, but I'm not sure if a Canadian one counts in the United States.

Chloe and I have been science partners since Grade Four, when her family moved to Corunna from

Winnipeg. We usually eat lunch together too. We'd probably be pretty good friends, except I'm always running for the ferry the minute the school bell rings. If you miss the boat to Centrelight, you're stuck on the mainland until the next one, which might be tomorrow. I tried that once when I was six—I wanted to hang around with some girls who were going to teach me to skip double Dutch. Dad had to come and rescue me with the Canada Customs boat, and I rode home on a shipment of impounded smelts. PS: smelt is a good name for those fish. My clothes "smelt" for six months, no matter how often we ran them through the washing machine.

I'm always whining to my folks about spending more time on the mainland. But the truth is I'm no more at home in Corunna than I am with Ronnie and that lot. I'd shame my dad into bringing me to a play date with Chloe and end up shivering in some ice rink, my teeth chattering over a cup of watery hot chocolate, watching her curling team out-sweep the competition. Whoop de doo.

So I don't fit in with the Michigan kids, but I don't really fit in on the mainland either, even if I were Aquaman and could swim over here any time

I wanted. I *thought* I fit in with Keenan. What a joke! I was good enough for his attention when he wasn't allowed to move off that lawn chair. But not anymore. Barney was my only *true* friend. And look what happened to him.

The boat ride back to Centrelight seems slower than ever—although what's my hurry? All I have to look forward to there is sitting in the cupola, doing homework and watching the rain.

When we finally dock and I'm walking across the platform, I'm surprised to see Barney Two running toward me, yipping and wagging. At first, I'm almost impressed. The real Barney used to meet me every day. The minute he heard the ferry's horn, there wasn't a leash or a fence that could hold him. This little twerp never had that kind of mojo—until today.

Then I look again. Barney Two is at the end of a leash—in Keenan's hand. That's probably the main reason he put up with me in the first place. He only liked me for my dog. Jerk.

Keenan is trying to melt into the crowd of parents meeting the boat. That way, when he gets in my face, I won't be able to ignore him.

"Save your breath, Keenan," I growl as I come into

range. "I don't want to hear it."

His manufactured smile disappears. "I left you a bunch of voicemails."

I play dumb. "A lot of calls get lost crossing the border." I march right past him and keep on going.

He follows me. Either that or it's Barney Two who's doing the following and Keenan's just being dragged behind.

"Come on, ZeeBee, wait up! This is important!"

I keep on walking. Then he blurts something that stops me in my tracks:

"I believe you that Barney was murdered!"

When I turn to face him, my fists are clenched and I can feel my cheeks radiating heat. "How low can you get?"

"No! ZeeBee! Listen—"

"Where do you get off using Barney to trick me into forgiving you? You *know* how much he meant to me!"

"But—"

I'm flaming at this point. "You're *worse* than Ronnie and those idiots! They're just brainless. You're a sleaze! When Barney died it was the worst day of my life. You ought to be ashamed of yourself."

"ZeeBee!"

I storm away in a towering rage. I'm moving at top

speed when Keenan catches up, jogging beside me.

"Don't forget your dog," he pants, handing me the leash.

That's another annoying thing about Barney Two. He's Keenan's way of always getting the last word.

15

Keenan

Shaggy fur, ranging from black to light brown, covers the entire animal, nose to tail, and right down to the webbed feet. He's a mutt, all right—probably a Heinz 57 variety. It's as if no two features come from the same dog breed—the hair of a sheepdog; the build of a Saint Bernard; the ears of an uncropped Doberman; the tail of an Australian shepherd; the paws of a Newfoundland; the body language of a pit bull.

For all that I've heard about the original Barney, I realize that I've never actually seen a picture of him. That's why I'm on ZeeBee's Instagram, where there are at least fifty of them—and not a single one of Barney Two, poor little guy. I browse through the gallery, examining the pet who stole ZeeBee's heart so totally that she can't even look at another dog.

Barney One is really something. I can't quite wrap my mind around the sheer size of him until I see this one snapshot where he's standing next to the Canada Customs jeep. The crown of his head is almost level with the roof of the vehicle.

I blink, and examine the photograph more closely. No, it's not a trick of perspective. ZeeBee always told me Barney was big, but wow. That's not a dog, it's a woolly mammoth!

It explains so much. I could never quite believe ZeeBee's stories about how much people hated Barney. So what? There are mischievous, troublemaking dogs everywhere. But when mischief comes in that size, it's terrifying. No wonder the police stopped responding to Barney calls. No wonder Animal Control wouldn't come to Centerlight from either Michigan or Ontario. I click on a video clip to play it. Barney, drenched and dripping, climbs out of the river. The wet hair on his face is slicked back, revealing his eyes. I've never seen an expression like that on anyone—human or animal—before. It's 100 percent wild, but it's more than that. Those are the eyes of a seeker, and what's being sought is trouble—as much as he can get into and as soon as possible. Then he shakes himself, and the spray is like Niagara Falls. Seriously, he could irrigate a whole field of crops. The water just keeps coming, even after a shower hits the camera lens and the video blurs.

I close ZeeBee's Instagram, but I can still see those eyes, staring at me, sizing me up, as if wondering how I'd taste. I turn away from the computer and the burning gaze actually follows me. Yeah, I get it now. This isn't the first time I doubted something ZeeBee told me only to have it turn out to be true.

If your goal was to take down Barney, of course you would have to use poison, because a rocket launcher might not be enough firepower to get the job done.

I'm ashamed of myself for that thought. ZeeBee is heartbroken over Barney. She *loved* him—so he couldn't have been all bad, because ZeeBee is a good person. And anyway, no matter how awful the dog might have been, the person who killed him is even more awful.

According to the dictionary, *murder* is the unlawful killing of another human. So I guess it doesn't count as that. But for sure it's some kind of crime. You can't go after people's pets just because they annoy you.

The more I think about it, the more it bugs me. Back during Prohibition, gangsters came to Centerlight and treated the law like it didn't apply to them. And now, decades later, some jerk with the same attitude thought it was fine to get rid of an old dog nobody liked, because nobody would care.

Well, *somebody* cares. ZeeBee cares. And as of now, so do I. Just because we aren't friends anymore doesn't mean I can't support her.

Some person—some *criminal*—is still walking around Centerlight, enjoying a Barney-free life, thinking he or she got away with murder.

We'll see about that!

I jump on my computer, ignoring the missed Skype call from Mom and Klaus. When you're dealing with a twelve-hour time difference, it's tough to find the right moment when everybody's awake and ready for small talk. Anyway, "How are you feeling, sweetie?" is not the question that interests me right now. What I care about is "Who killed Barney?"

I find the website of the Centerlight *Islander,* and

search the archives. I start with the keyword *police calls*. Although this used to be the gangster capital of North America, the crime situation is pretty different now. A couple of homeowners got tickets for planting bamboo in their yards—it grows too fast and messes up people's septic tanks. A bunch of tourists misplaced their wallets and thought they'd been robbed. One lady was arrested because she didn't pay her speeding tickets. There was even a guy who got in trouble for having too many overdue library books.

I refine my search, adding *dog* to the other keywords. That's when I strike gold.

POOCH PUMMELS PORSCHE INTO PORCH

On warm nights, Michael Farnsworth of Abbot Street leaves the sunroof of his new Porsche open to let in the fresh air. It's something he will never do again.

Last Wednesday evening, a large dog climbed in through the roof opening in order to reach the candy bar Mr. Farnsworth had left in the cup holder. The dog, having made short work of the candy, found himself unable to squeeze back out through the roof. Howling and barking, the agitated animal tore up the leather seats and destroyed the interior of the car as he struggled to free himself. His efforts cracked the windshield and dislodged the parking brake, causing the Porsche to roll down the slope. The car collided with the wraparound porch of the Farnsworth home, knocking out the support struts, and collapsing a section of roof. The insurance company estimates the damage in excess of $50,000.

The dog has been identified as Barney Tice, belonging to the family of Officer Darryl Tice, a Canadian Border officer . . .

I skim through the rest of it. Even after his harrowing experience, Barney still had the strength to bulldoze his way through the damaged passenger door, sending it at least ten feet clear of the wreckage. And—I check the date of the article on my screen—this supposedly happened on April 16. According to ZeeBee, the morning of April 18 was when they found Barney dead. Does that sound like a dog within forty-eight hours of the end of his natural life? Barney had to smell the candy through its wrapper, climb up onto the roof, squeeze into the car, and literally blast his way out. It wouldn't get him on the dean's list at obedience school, but it wouldn't put him at death's door either. I have a murky vision of the gaping hole in the Lindahls' fence—another recent incident. Sure, Barney was no puppy, but he was *healthy*. He didn't die of natural causes. He had help!

My eyes narrow at the grainy photograph of Michael Farnsworth. Does he seem like the kind of person who would poison a dog? He definitely doesn't look happy, but neither would I if I was watching the tow truck hauling what's left of my car away from what's left of my house.

I dig deeper. The crime stories in the *Islander*'s archives detail a variety of minor offenses that could have come from any tourist town our size. But the dog complaints are *all* Barney. I mean 100 percent. You would think there weren't any other dogs on Centerlight. He dug up gardens; he damaged property; he scared children; he disturbed the peace; he stopped traffic; he terrorized cats; he chewed through wires; he used anywhere and everywhere as his personal toilet.

He operated on both sides of the border. He had every bit as much enthusiasm for damaging American property as Canadian. Some of the victims are people I know—like Ronnie's family, and the Quayle sisters, and that writer, Mr. Tolenski. I guess when you're trying to research a book, the last thing you need is a giant dog howling down the neighborhood. Some of the articles go back a decade or even more.

Mr. Chaiken, the grocer, filed sixteen separate complaints—and those were just the ones that made the paper. The *Islander* reporters never ran out of headlines to describe Barney's attacks on the store's cheese display: MUENSTER MAULED, CHEDDAR CHEWED, ROQUEFORT RANSACKED, BRIE BITTEN, SWISS SLURPED, PROVOLONE PURLOINED. Barney cost Mr. Chaiken a lot of money over the years. He must have been desperate. The real question is: Was he desperate enough to poison a dog?

It's impossible to tell from old newspaper articles. The truth is, every single one of the victims had good reason to want to be rid of Barney. ZeeBee said it herself: Everybody hated him.

This is a real crime. To get to the bottom of it, I'm going to have to think like a detective.

When I enter the office, Dr. Hirschorn looks at me and then looks directly behind me. At first, I think there's something wrong with his eyesight. After a minute, I realize that he's trying to locate the animal I must have brought with me. Who else would go to a vet?

"Oh no, I don't have a pet," I tell him.

"Then you've come to the wrong place, son," he

deadpans. "We don't carry a flea collar in your size."

He seems to expect me to laugh at that, so I do. The thing is, Dr. Hirschorn was *Barney's* vet, so he's the guy to ask whether or not his former patient died of natural causes.

"You looked after Barney, right?" I venture. "The Tices' dog?"

"Every dog. Every pet," he confirms. "I'm the only vet on the island. Sure, I know Barney. Cute little spaniel."

"No, I mean the *real* Barney." I catch myself using ZeeBee's words and rephrase. "The *first* one."

"Oh. *That* Barney." The vet's eyes open wide at the memory. He rolls up his sleeve to reveal a semicircle of small scars. "See this? Bite mark. Teeth like a grizzly. Barney didn't appreciate shots."

"But he *had* all his shots, right?" I seize on that. "He was under a vet's care and he was healthy?"

Dr. Hirschorn shrugs. "Couldn't have been that healthy. He's dead, isn't he?"

"That's the confusing part. He was active and strong. He broke out of a car; blasted through a fence—"

"Don't forget the time he trashed my examining room," the vet adds. "Knocked my assistant unconscious. I lost more employees thanks to that dog—"

162

"Does that sound like an animal on the verge of dying of old age?" I interrupt.

He spreads his hands. "Fifteen is a lot of years for a dog that size. Who knows?"

I stare at him. "Don't you?"

"Listen, son. The only sure way to determine cause of death is a necropsy—that's what we call an autopsy for animals. Nobody does all that for a fifteen-year-old dog."

"But what if it was, you know, foul play?"

"What foul play?" An expression of understanding comes over his face. "You're a friend of the daughter's, right?"

I'm not in the mood to go into how ZeeBee hates me, so I just say, "I have reason to believe Barney was poisoned."

The vet leans back in his swivel chair and folds his arms in front of him. "Look, this isn't a tragedy. The dog had a long life and a family that loved him. Let's leave it at that, okay?"

"Okay," I agree reluctantly. "But can you totally rule out the possibility that Barney's cause of death was poisoning?"

"One hundred percent? Not without a necropsy." He adds, "You're obviously new around here. There's no foul play on Centerlight. We didn't even get cell service until 2007. If you're looking for intrigue, you came to the wrong place."

I almost argue with him, but I know it won't do any good. What the vet's *really* saying is that Barney isn't worth investigating because he was just a dog.

No wonder ZeeBee is so bitter. I'm starting to feel pretty bitter myself.

But I get one thing out of Dr. Hirschorn: He never said Barney *wasn't* poisoned; just that he didn't think so. And if he's wrong, there are plenty of suspects who had motive to want Barney out of the picture.

16

Zarabeth

My patience for school keeps getting lower and lower. Once lunch is over, I basically spend the rest of the day staring at the clock, trying to use telekinetic power to move the hands forward to three thirty. And for what? So I can sprint to the ferry terminal and be the first one on board? I still have to wait for the slowest kindergartner to get dragged the three blocks by his mother or nanny before we can all cast off for Centrelight.

It's a pointless routine, yet I can't stop repeating it, day after day. It's all Keenan's fault. When we were friends, I was always anxious to finish what I was doing so we could get together. Now we're not friends anymore, but I'm still anxious to get finished. And do what? Rush home to Centrelight so I can be bored there? Phooey!

Today I get to the dock to find the Canada Customs patrol boat bobbing in the water next to the ferry. Dad is there, waving at me. "Hop in, ZeeBee. I'll give you a ride home."

Well, this day is starting to look up. No ferry ride with smoke and whining kids and high schoolers nuzzling each other behind the bulkheads. So I'm smiling when I jump aboard and we head out across the river.

I'm not smiling about thirty seconds later when he hands me an official-looking document with the Canadian government logo on the top.

I frown. "What's this about?"

"I could ask you the same question," he replies grimly. "This came across my desk this morning."

I study the document. It's a robbery report on a green CCM mountain bike that's been missing for three weeks. Under *Complainant*, it says *Anonymous call to tip line.*

"What do you have to say for yourself?"

"The people in your office are terrible .typists," I complain. "That's not how you spell *larceny*."

He doesn't appreciate my joke. "That's Wayne's bike, isn't it? And the anonymous tipster—that's you."

"I'm looking out for my brother." I try to brazen it through. "Just because he's in Toronto doesn't mean we should let his stuff get ripped off."

"Who do you think you're talking to, ZeeBee? We both know Keenan has Wayne's bike."

"That makes it even worse," I argue. "A foreigner committed a crime on Canadian soil and took the proceeds across an international frontier. A border officer should understand how serious that is!"

"Give it a rest. You loaned Keenan that bike. Why are you stirring up trouble for the poor kid? If I hadn't seen this, he could have been arrested."

"Don't you mean arrested *again*?" I demand.

"He wasn't arrested the first time."

"Too bad," I snort. "Arrest was invented for back-stabbers like him."

Dad sighs. "I can't pick your friends, but it seems to me that you and Keenan were getting along just fine before that night at the lighthouse. He's an okay kid. What did he do to you to make you so mad?"

I don't answer. It's nothing I could ever explain to Dad. I don't know if I really understand it myself. Mad isn't something you get to choose whether or not you want to be. It just happens.

I tear up the paper and give it a burial at sea. "Keenan isn't going to get into any actual trouble, is he?" I ask Dad. "You know, by accident."

"I'm not stupid," he tells me. "I deleted the complaint from our system before coming to get you. I even wiped the phone message from the tip line. Were you talking into a paper bag?"

"A Dixie cup," I admit. Dad's a better detective than I thought. Canada is in good hands with guys like him guarding our borders.

His shift is still on, so he drops me on Centrelight and heads back out on the river. As I make my way across Laurier/Jefferson Park, I notice the usual gang of idiots from the middle school horsing around with one of those giant beach balls.

I squint at the faces. Keenan isn't with them. Come to think of it, I haven't seen him with that after-school crowd for a few days now.

I wonder where he's been going.

17

Keenan

Michael Farnsworth bought a new Porsche after Barney trashed the old one, and the porch of his home has been fixed. The porch is important, because that's my excuse for knocking on his door.

"I'm doing a school project on island architecture," I explain when he answers. "I notice a lot of people have wraparound porches. Yours looks brand-new. Did you just add it to the house?"

His expression hardens. "It's a repair. After an insurance claim."

"Looks great," I assure him. "So the idea of my project is that Centerlighters like porches because there are so many water views around. Would you agree with that?"

He seems impatient. "Yeah, sure. Why not? Mind you, I didn't have a lot of choice but to redo it. It was toothpicks."

"Toothpicks?" I take out a notebook and pencil. "What happened?"

He shrugs. "You don't want to listen to that whole sob story."

"Of course I do. These are the details that will make my project interesting. Did one of these big trees fall on it?" Obviously, I know exactly what damaged his porch. But I want to hear how he describes it.

"If you must know, a car hit it."

I glance over my shoulder to the road. "A car came all the way over here? That driver must have been really out of control."

"It wasn't a driver." He's tight-lipped. "It was—a dog."

I pretend I didn't hear. "Sorry?"

"A dog," he says, louder. "A dog drove my car into

my house. Well, he didn't *drive*, exactly. He——"

Inside, the phone rings. Mr. Farnsworth is flustered. "Listen, come in for a second. We're air-conditioning the street."

I follow him inside. He answers the phone, and gets into a conversation about stocks and bonds, signaling for me to wait as he ducks into the next room for privacy.

I'm alone in the sunny, modern kitchen. I experience a moment of indecision. I got myself into the house, but what next? I can't very well come out and accuse him of poisoning Barney. Maybe he didn't do it. Sure, he had plenty of reason to hate the dog, but so did a lot of people.

I could keep asking about the accident, hoping that he gets so worked up against Barney that he confesses. But if I lay it on too thick, he'll just kick me out. Then I'm back to square one. This is harder than I thought.

Desperately, I look around the kitchen. I have no idea what I expect to find—a framed confession: *I killed the dog*?

My eyes fall on a calendar hanging beside one of the cabinets. I don't know why it occurs to me to turn back the pages. Maybe it's the dates in that old newspaper article: April 16—the accident with the Porsche/

porch; April 18—Barney discovered dead.

I flip to April. The sixteenth and eighteenth are both clear. But—the seventeenth is circled in red magic marker!

My heart begins to pound. If the Tices found Barney on the morning of April 18, then the seventeenth must have been the day the poisoning took place!

"Hey!" Mr. Farnsworth is back in the kitchen, regarding me suspiciously. "What do you want with my calendar?"

In full detective mode, I wheel on him. "Where were you on the night of April seventeenth?"

He stares at me. "What kind of a school project is this?"

"Why is that date circled in red?" I persist.

Now I have no trouble reading his signs. His cheeks flame red. His eyes shoot sparks. He's angry, and not at any dog. At me.

"Get out of my house, and take your school project with you. Crazy kid!"

Ten seconds later, I'm out on the street, and Mr. Farnsworth is an even stronger suspect than before.

But I don't think he'll be answering any of my questions again.

★ ★ ★

Elspeth Quayle pours me a cup of tea—Earl Grey. "Now tell me about this project you're working on, young man."

I take a sip and practically gag. The Quayle sisters, who live on the Canadian side, seem like the sweetest, most harmless little old ladies on the face of the earth. But they drink a toxic brew that could take the paint off Wayne's bicycle.

"So," I rasp, sucking air in an attempt to soothe my burned tongue, "it's a profile for our school paper on the winners of the Centerlight Garden Show for the last twelve years straight."

The two sisters are so pleased their buttons practically pop. Muriel Quayle sprinkles water on a row of immaculate white roses. "How sweet of you to recognize our accomplishment. The Canadian Horticultural Society has named this variety the Quayle rose."

"You'll want to mention that in your story," her sister puts in.

I pretend to write it down in my notebook. "I guess what I'm most interested in," I tell them, "are the problems you had to overcome to win so many—uh—flower championships."

"It's a struggle," Miss Muriel agrees. "How did we

ever make it through 2010? The year of the greenfly. I don't think I slept a night all summer."

"Yeah, but bigger animals gave you problems too, right?"

Miss Elspeth nods tragically. "Grasshoppers. Oh, how we suffered. Those monsters can eat a garden bare."

"Actually," I say, "I was thinking of something even bigger than that. Like—a dog?"

The change in the two ladies is instant and dramatic. It's not like they start yelling and cursing or anything like that. Actually, they get even quieter. But both faces drain of all color until they resemble vampires except for the spots of rouge decorating ash-white cheeks.

"There was a dog," Miss Muriel practically whispers. "A deplorable animal. Mother raised us to believe that no living creature was beyond all hope, but Mother never knew Barney."

"He had a taste for our roses." Miss Elspeth takes up the tale. "What he didn't eat, he rolled in—or worse. His defiance was almost human. It wasn't enough for him to destroy our garden. He had to wave in our faces the fact that there was nothing we could do to stop him. No fence could keep him out. He could get into any greenhouse, even if he had to smash every pane of glass. And when there was nothing left save a few crumpled petals, he would stand amid the wreckage, taunting us through the windows."

I look around the property. Lush green is everywhere. Roses, asters, and chrysanthemums provide explosions of color even this late into the fall. The greenhouse gleams like a jewel.

"It all looks really good now," I comment. "How did you get that dog to stop coming?"

"Fate stopped him," Miss Muriel supplies, sounding a little bit too pleased. "Our tormentor is dead. And heaven forgive me, I'm not sorry."

"Heaven forgives you," her sister assures her. "He was just that dreadful."

"Actually, I think I've heard of the dog you're talking about," I comment as if the idea just occurred to me. "You know, some people think he was poisoned."

"Well, obviously," Miss Muriel says, "we wouldn't know anything about that."

"Do you ladies happen to remember what you were doing on April seventeenth?" I venture.

Miss Elspeth shakes her head sadly. "My memory isn't what it used to be."

"Don't be silly, Elspeth," her sister interrupts. "Of

course you remember. That was the date of the big meeting at the community hall—the one about funding the repairs to the lighthouse. The whole town was there."

My mind races. These islanders and their lighthouse! The Americans and the Canadians are equally obsessed with it. Mr. Farnsworth—is that why he had April 17 circled on his calendar? Of course, just because you're at a town meeting doesn't mean you don't have plenty of time to poison a dog. In fact, the meeting could provide the killer with a golden opportunity. He—or she—could slip out of a crowded hearing room, do the deed, and slip back in without being noticed.

I hang out with the sisters for another ten minutes, gagging down some more of that tea so I don't offend them. It isn't lava hot anymore, so now the flavors come through. Warm perfume.

They talk my ear off about the science of blossom color and the perfect pH of soil. The sisters are so genuinely sweet and boring that it's hard to picture them hurting Barney. Then I remember how different they were while talking about the damage he did to their garden and I'm not so sure.

As they show me out of the yard, we pass a shelf that holds containers of fertilizer and plant food, and some metal hand tools. In the center is a dark glass bottle half full of liquid. The label has a large skull and cross-bones on it. That can only mean one thing.

Poison.

My next stop is the community hall.

It's more or less a town hall. But they don't call it that since Centerlight is technically two separate towns, one in Michigan and the other in Ontario. Both share this facility, which is housed in an old mansion on the Canadian side. ZeeBee once told me it used to be owned by Arnold Rothstein, the legendary gangster who fixed the 1919 World Series.

The first thing I notice is the location. It's practically kitty-corner to the Tices' house, on the other side of an empty lot. Which means someone at the meeting could have slipped out and been just a few dozen steps away from Barney.

The place was probably really elegant back in the day, but now it's just an old pile that smells a lot like the river—kind of damp and musty. It's not really a government building so much as a collection of island archives and public meeting rooms.

I tell the one and only clerk that I'm doing a school project on the lighthouse. If the people on this island ever get together and compare notes on all the projects I'm supposedly working on, I'm toast.

"I heard there was a big meeting about it here on April seventeenth," I tell her. "Are there any, you know, records I could look over?"

Wordlessly, she turns her back on me and disappears into a side room. She's gone for so long that I actually start to wonder if maybe she left for the day. But then she returns with a thick file that she slaps onto the counter in front of me. "Help yourself."

The technology level in the community hall hasn't changed much since Arnold Rothstein's time. I haven't seen a single computer yet. When I lug the file over to a table and open it, my worst fears come true. It's all handwritten in a scribbly cursive that's borderline unreadable. I actually groan a little, and the clerk looks over in sympathy.

I sit down and try to plow through it. As near as I can tell, they met for over three hours, and issued a statement that they all love the lighthouse. But six million dollars is a lot of money for a community the size of Centerlight. They're willing to raise some of it if the government picks up the rest. But which government? The U.S.A.? Canada? Michigan? Ontario? In the end, the only thing everyone would agree on was to meet in another six months to try again.

By this time, my eyes are bugging out of my head from decoding all those chicken scratches. The next page is even worse—at least twenty different examples of handwriting, maybe more. Then I realize what I'm looking at. It's the sign-in sheet—signatures and addresses of everyone at the meeting. I flip forward. Six pages of names. I spy the Quayle sisters and—yes, there's Mr. Farnsworth. There's a Harry Chaiken, who must be the grocer. I wonder how many more of these people are Barney-haters with a motive for murder. A quick glance over my shoulder. The clerk is off in the corner, making a fresh pot of coffee. I whip out my phone and photograph all six sign-in sheets. This is probably against the rules, but I need these names and addresses. Every single one of these people was right near the Tice house the night Barney was poisoned.

I thank the clerk and just about fall over my feet getting out of there. On the way home, the wheels of Wayne's bike barely touch the ground.

"Hey, kid." My father is in the kitchen, gazing at something charcoal black in a roasting pan. "Pizza sound good tonight? Had a little mishap with the chicken."

"Sure, Dad. I've just got some stuff to do first."

Upstairs in my room, I sit at my computer, my phone next to the keyboard. One by one, I take all the Barney complaints from the Centerlight *Islander* and check them against the attendees of the big meeting back in April. Those are the people who go on my list of suspects: the ones with both motive *and* opportunity.

FARNSWORTH, MICHAEL: Local finance bigwig. Grievance: Trashed Porsche and porch.

BATISTA, ARABELLA: Opera singer. Grievance: Howling threw her off-key.

STICKLE, MARTIN: Avid cyclist. Grievance: Barney hunted everything on two wheels.

CHAIKEN, HARRY: Grocer. Grievance: Grand theft cheddar.

PICCOLI, VINCENT AND LOLA: Retirees. Grievance: Their yard was ground zero for Barney's digging habit.

TOLENSKI, PETER: Writer. Grievance: Barking made work impossible.

QUAYLE, ELSPETH AND MURIEL: Flower geniuses. Grievance: Rose-icide

LINDAHL, DOUGLAS: Ronnie's dad. Grievance: 1 fence plus several ransacked barbecues.

PING, LEON: Cat owner. Grievance: His tabby, Fagan, was Barney's arch-nemesis.

I print the page and sit back, examining it with great concentration. These nine possibilities cover everyone who 1) was at that April 17 meeting and 2) once filed a police complaint against Barney. I'm positive the name of the killer is on the list somewhere.

I fight down the urge to rush over to ZeeBee's house and show her how much I've learned. She'd be impressed, grateful even. Then we could make up and get to work solving this together.

But I have to face facts: She doesn't want anything to do with me.

18

Zarabeth

Keenan is up to something, but I can't figure out what.

Okay, I've been spying on him. Sue me. Half my DNA comes from a border officer, so I'm genetically predisposed to snoop.

Besides, it's not my fault Keenan makes it so easy. Like clockwork, every Wednesday and Saturday he's at Island Fitness for his workouts with that Bryce musclehead. So I always know exactly where to find him.

Then yesterday, he spent forty-five minutes in the community hall when it's a fact that nothing in that dump could hold your interest for forty-five seconds. I timed him from my usual spot in the cupola. And when he finally came out, that left eyebrow of his was three-quarters of the way to the moon. What was he doing in there?

I don't mind mysteries, but I really hate not knowing what's going on.

I could just ask him. But that would mean I'd have to talk to him, which is *not* going to happen. I've imposed sanctions on Keenan. He probably doesn't care or even notice, which is annoying. I've thought about explaining it to him, but in order to do that, I'd have to break my own sanctions.

So on Saturday, I duck behind a pickup truck in the Tim Horton's parking lot, waiting for him to come out of Island Fitness. (Only in Centrelight can you hide in Canada while staking out someone in the United States.)

Barney Two dances around my ankles, yipping up at me questioningly, as if asking what the game is. Annoyed, I reach out my toe and nudge him into the cover of the truck with me. "Keep quiet, dummy," I murmur.

Eventually, Keenan emerges from the gym and gets on his (Wayne's) bike. I hop on my own and follow at a distance, Barney Two hot on my heels. I stay off the main road, sticking to the alleyway behind the shops. I can't let Keenan see me. That might give him the idea that I recognize the fact that he's alive, which would definitely be a violation of the sanctions.

Sure enough, Keenan rides right past the turnoff for his dad's house. Just as I suspected, he's not going home. He's been all over the island lately, which only adds to the mystery.

That ends today. My plan is to follow him and figure out where he's going and why.

When the alley runs out, I switch to a parallel street, catching glimpses of him between homes. I have no worry about keeping up. Wayne's bike hasn't been oiled since he got his driver's license two years ago.

I follow him through a couple of turns, always keeping a street away. We haven't ridden very much farther when he stops reappearing after every house. That can only mean one thing. He's reached his destination. I turn on the afterburners, whip around the block to the main road, and approach cautiously, dismounting and walking my bike, shielded by a tall hedge. Sure enough, there's Wayne's green CCM parked in the driveway of a neat Cape Cod–style home. Barney Two catches up, panting happily. I can't explain why, but the fact that he gets such a charge out of everything I do really irritates me.

I frown at the house. The place is kind of familiar, but I can't quite remember who lives there. It's frustrating, because I pride myself on knowing pretty much everybody on the island, even on the American side. I'm pretty sure it isn't one of the kids from the middle school.

And then a head pokes out of the bushes behind me—yellow eyes, tiger stripes, short fur, long whiskers. I jump at the sight of him. It's Fagan, the Cat from the Black Lagoon! That's why I recognize this place. It's Leon Ping's house!

Fagan lets out an unfriendly yowl that passes for his sick version of a meow. Suddenly, a blond shape interposes itself between the cat and me. I'm amazed. It's Barney Two, and here's proof that he's actually dumber than I thought he was. Not even the real Barney would mess with Fagan, and Barney wasn't afraid of anybody—man, woman, or beast. This little cocker nothing is about to get sliced into bacon strips!

What Fagan does next is the last thing I expect: He *purrs*. Barney Two approaches, wagging and sniffing.

They touch noses. It's enough to make you throw up. They're practically bonding. Fagan doesn't bond. He slashes you to pieces!

The feud between my Barney and this awful cat was the greatest rivalry on Centrelight since Al Capone versus the FBI. Barney would shred Fagan's cat toys and Fagan would respond by going all the way to Canada and using Barney's supper dish as a litter box. And when it got physical, Fagan would carve Barney up like an Easter ham, even though Barney outweighed him by about 2,000 percent.

As if that wasn't bad enough, Mr. Ping would call the cops—on *Barney*, who practically needed a blood transfusion after these battles. Talk about unfair!

So why is Keenan visiting this jackass? Why would they even know each other?

Keenan's inside the house for about twenty minutes. When he finally comes out, he and Mr. Ping are still talking. I'd give anything to hear what they're saying, but I'm too far away. They shake hands and Keenan heads for Wayne's bike.

I back away into the shadow of the hedge, pulling my stupid dog away from his new best friend. "Traitor!" I hiss into his furry ear.

What else would you call someone who's been caught fraternizing with the other side?

Keenan's next stop is a home on the next street over from mine. Even if I didn't remember the house itself, I'd instantly recognize the property. The giant holes in the lawn would tell me that this is where Barney used to bury his bones and other treasures—toys, old shoes, candlesticks, legs broken off pieces of furniture, someone's crutch, an oar, an umbrella, a goalie pad. The list goes on and on. Mr. Piccoli, who lives here, once claimed that he found an entire crystal chandelier entombed in his yard. In order to get it as deep as he said, Barney would have had to bite through a cable wire and rupture a gas line, which could have taken out the whole neighborhood. But I don't believe it. I went on the internet and sure enough, no one reported a missing chandelier.

I can see Keenan in the house, chatting up the Piccolis. Mrs. Piccoli is pouring him a glass of juice or iced tea or something.

First Mr. Ping and now this. A pattern is beginning to emerge—a *Barney* pattern.

While I'm staring in the window, trying to make

sense of it, Barney Two scampers onto the lawn, jumps into one of the holes, and emerges with what looks like a shank bone. He trots over and drops it proudly at my feet.

I well up with emotion. This is from Barney. Not *this* Barney; *my* Barney—the real one. I stuff it in my pocket. It might be the last thing from him I'll ever touch.

Keenan's next destination doesn't ring a bell until I peer into the open garage and see the bikes hanging on the wall. There are six of them, all racers, all super expensive. I know this because we once had to pay for one. The frame got bent when Barney knocked the cyclist off it with a flying tackle. The bike was ruined. My parents said we were lucky the rider—this guy Martin Stickle—wasn't ruined too.

We thought Barney was sick that night because he was wheezing. The next thing we knew, he coughed up a swatch of fluorescent nylon. He was fine after that, but we couldn't figure out where the fabric came from. Mr. Stickle showed up at our door first thing in the morning, holding the bicycle shorts with the hole bitten out of the seat. What was left of his bike was in the trunk of his car. If we needed more proof, he offered to show us the condition of his butt cheek. (Dad said we'd take his word for it.)

I told Mr. Stickle that the incident was half his fault for wearing such flashy clothes. Animals are attracted to bright colors; that's why a bull can't resist a matador's red cape. He replied that no raging bull was half the threat to life and limb as Barney, and threatened to sue. Dad got him calmed down by offering to buy a new bike and pay his doctor bills.

That same Mr. Stickle is now in the garage with Keenan, showing him the different bikes. Keenan has a notebook out and he's writing things down. Like he's a reporter or something! What gives?

Barney Two is nuzzling my ankle and I nudge him out of range with my sneaker. Why are you interviewing this creep, Keenan? Don't you realize how much trouble he made for my family? Just like the Piccolis, who took us to court even after Dad bought an entire truckload of topsoil for their stupid lawn. Or Mr. Ping, who called Animal Control on Barney, when it was his psycho cat that really needed controlling.

It's bad enough that Keenan dropped me like a hot potato the minute he started hanging out with those mouth-breathers from the middle school. But this is even worse.

I turn it over in my mind every which way, but there's only one possible explanation: He's going out of his way to make friends with everyone on the island who hates my family. I think of the mysterious footsteps, and car engines, and voices I hear outside my house when I'm trying to fall asleep at night. I picture that boot print that's too big to have come from my dad.

Maybe those things aren't so mysterious after all. We have *enemies*, and their newest member is named Keenan Cardinal.

He's plotting against me!

19

Ronnie

My folks keep an oil painting of my great-grand-father, Pierce Ronald Lindahl III—barf—in the place of honor over the mantel in the library. It's a quirk of our house that if you slam the front door too hard, that picture falls off the hook, hits the floor, and busting the frame.

It's annoying, but it's also a good early warning system for when Dad is really steamed about something. As soon as I hear the *slam-crash-crack* I go on red alert.

Not that it helps. We've got a big house, but he always finds me anyway.

"Ronnie!"

I peek out from the top of the steps. "Hey, Dad. How was work?"

"Get your butt down here!"

Wouldn't it be great if I could stay upstairs and send only my butt to get yelled at? It doesn't work that way.

I meet him in the front hall. "What's up, Dad?" I mean, besides your blood pressure.

"What's the name of that friend of yours?" he begins. "The new kid—Connor, Kenny . . ."

"You mean Keenan?"

"Whatever his name is. Do you know he called me at the office today? Did you give him my number?"

"Of course not." I'm pretty blown away. Why would Keenan want to talk to my dad? Although I do remember us talking once about where our fathers work. "What did he say?"

"That's the weirdest part. He kept asking about that demon dog—the one that put a hole in our fence. What's up with that?"

"Beats me," I say honestly. "He's friends with Zoo-doo, so maybe that's the connection. Barney was her dog."

His eyes narrow. "You're leaving something out, Ronnie. Whenever something screwy happens around here, you're usually at the bottom of it."

Okay, that's probably true. But not in this case. "Honest, I'm as clueless as you are. Why would Keenan care about some dead mutt? And why call you when he could just ask me at school?"

He wags a warning finger under my nose. "You stay away from this kid. He's not quite right in the head. He kept asking me where I was on some day back in April. How should I know?"

I'm mystified. "Keenan wasn't even here in April. He was in China. Or was it Lesotho . . ."

"Don't you start." Dad cuts me off. "Just tell Kenny to lose my number. I'm trying to run a business here. I don't have time to waste on some twelve-year-old nutjob." He storms off into the library to rehang Great-Grandpa.

I stand there in the hallway, shaking my head. What's with Keenan? I mean, who calls someone's *dad*—at work—to talk about a dead dog? I wouldn't hit up his old man to talk about anything.

Come to think of it, outside of school, Keenan hasn't been hanging out as much these days. He wouldn't come to my ironman contest, where we set fire to pieces of driftwood and see who can dance on them the longest before burning their feet. And he blew off Joey's Splat Night, which is when we throw rotten crabapples down on cars crossing the bridge. Who would miss out on good times like that?

So what's the deal with Keenan? I haven't seen him with Zoo-doo, so he probably isn't spending all his time with her. I feel like I know him, but the truth is I don't really know him at all.

I keep picturing him on the phone with Dad. The fence. The dog. Some day this past April.

No matter how much I rack my brain, none of it makes any sense.

He's definitely up to something. But what?

20

Keenan

It's kind of cool to be running an investigation in a place where history's greatest cops investigated history's most notorious criminals.

Okay, I get it—I sound like ZeeBee. But just because she's obsessed doesn't mean she's always wrong. Barney really *was* murdered—even if it doesn't count as murder in the legal sense. And as I put together the pieces of how it happened, I can't help thinking of guys like Eliot Ness, who once stood on this very island, gathering evidence just like I'm doing.

It's a long way from Shanghai—and not just on a map. To be honest, I hardly ever think about my old life anymore. When Mom and Klaus Skype me, I'm just going through the motions: *Hey, how's it going? Fine. How about you? Blah, blah, blah . . .*

"All right," Mom says suddenly. "Out with it."

"Out with what?" I ask.

"There's something you're not telling me," she accuses. "Are you sick again?"

That's another thing about me now. I'm not over-tired. I'm not out of breath. I still can't land that tae kwon do kick with Bryce, but otherwise I'm really good. It's the investigation that's put me over the top. I've felt fine for a while, but you're not really back to normal until you forget to think about how you feel.

"I'm great," I tell her.

"You seem distracted."

Mom's right about that. While talking to Mom, I'm mentally replaying my attempt to question Arabella Batista, the opera singer. I went to her house, armed with the usual excuse about interviewing her for a school project. I could hear her inside, playing the piano and singing. I rang the bell, and the music stopped—but nobody came to the door.

I rang again. Nothing.

I walked around the side of the house and actually saw her silhouette through the lace curtains—a tall figure, powerfully built, with shoulders like a nose tackle. She was still at the piano, motionless, as if waiting for the person at the door to go away.

Obviously, she doesn't like to be disturbed while she's singing. The question is: How far would she go to keep herself from being disturbed by a howling dog?

"Keenan . . . *Keenan!*" Mom's sharp voice jars me out of the memory and back to my room.

"Sorry, Mom. You were saying . . . ?"

She seems annoyed. "I said do you want me to talk to your father about seeing another doctor for a second opinion? I'm sure Dr. Sobel's very good, but I'm starting to think he might be dragging his feet about letting you come home."

Home. The word echoes in my brain, sung out in Ms. Batista's powerful soprano. Sure, I miss Mom, and Klaus, and my friends. So why isn't the idea of going back to Shanghai more appealing to me?

For starters, I'm not restless anymore, and I'm definitely not bored. Just the opposite—I'm totally wrapped up in the search for Barney's killer. It's like it's taken over my mind to the point where I don't have spare brain cells to waste on anything else.

Besides, define home. The longest Mom and Klaus ever stay in the same city is about a year. Those places always seem strange at first, but after a while, they start to feel like home. Well, that can happen just as easily with Centerlight.

"I don't need a second opinion," I reply finally. "I'm good—seriously. It isn't Shanghai, but there's actually a lot going on around here."

Mom is satisfied with that, and I manage to get her off Skype. But when I said "a lot going on," I really meant the investigation. Endless details, endless possibilities.

The pair of heavy heat-resistant gloves I saw by the firepit in the Lindahl backyard. They're designed to keep you from getting burned. But wouldn't they also protect a would-be killer from a nasty dog bite?

Did Mr. Ping use Fagan to lure Barney to the poisoned meat? Or is Mr. Chaiken the most obvious culprit because he's a grocer, with an unlimited supply of steaks?

The names swirl before me—Farnsworth, Batista, Stickle, Piccoli, Tolenski, Quayle—along with the one motive they share: *revenge.*

Eliot Ness had it easy. His gangsters were all guilty and the only problem was proving it. But the Barney evidence points equally to everybody. And the more suspects I talk to, the muddier the picture gets.

I approach Mr. Tolenski at Island Fitness, since his time slot with Bryce comes right after mine.

"Ah, the black belt," he says when he recognizes me.

I laugh. "More like no belt. I'm lucky I can keep my pants up. How's the book coming along?"

He shrugs. "The book writes itself at its own speed. I'm just the instrument."

"I never thought about it that way." That gives me an opening. "Hey, for school, we're supposed to do a report on someone we know with an interesting job. Would you let me interview you?"

He looks over at Bryce. "Okay if I give the kid a few minutes?"

Bryce nods. "My five o'clock is running late. You should be fine."

We sit down at a bench just beyond the weight machines. I start out by asking a few questions about where he gets his ideas. Not because I care, but if I start interrogating him about big, loud dogs straight out of the gate, he's going to know I'm after information about Barney. He rambles on about how you don't choose your topic; the topic chooses you. Yawn.

"What are the biggest problems you've faced as a writer?" I probe.

"Only one," he replies. "Myself. My book is out there in the world, waiting for me to access it. The only person who can get in the way of that is me."

"But what about distractions?" I persist. "Dripping faucets? Noisy neighbors? Dogs?"

He frowns. "Dogs?"

I play my trump card. "You know that lady, Miss Batista? She sings with the Oakland County Opera. She said there was a big dog on the island who howled every time she tried to rehearse. That could be pretty annoying to a writer too."

He smiles. "Did your opera singer ever consider the fact that it was her voice that was distracting to the dog and not vice versa?"

Bryce comes over. "Sorry, Clark Kent. You're starting to run into Mr. T's workout time."

Mr. Tolenski shoots the trainer a mock scolding look. "It was just starting to get interesting."

I stand up. "I've got everything I need—really. Thanks, Mr. Tolenski!"

As I bike home from Island Fitness, something about

the interview keeps gnawing at me. Maybe it's this: Mr. Tolenski is good at *sounding* like this genius writer, with statements like "Your topic chooses you" and "I'm just the instrument." But he never talks about what he's actually writing. He's supposedly working on this book about Centerlight's criminal past, but he didn't say a word about his research. Contrast that with ZeeBee, who isn't writing anything, and never shuts up about gangsters for a minute.

Come to think of it, how can I be so sure that Mr. Tolenski is a real writer? I've never seen any of his books before, and neither has anyone I've ever mentioned him to. And if he's being dishonest about his job, it brings up the question of what other sleazy and nefarious things he might be involved in.

I get home and pound up the stairs, totally amped to prove that Mr. Tolenski is a giant fraud. In my investigation, I've been learning a lot of important information about my suspects. What *I haven't* been learning is anything that would help me eliminate any of them. In order to find out who poisoned Barney, I have to go from nine suspects to one.

That could happen today. If Mr. Tolenski is lying about being a writer, he'd automatically shoot up to the top of the suspect list.

I jump on my computer and do a Google search for the keywords *Peter Tolenski* and *writer*.

What appears on the screen is the Amazon page for something called *The Fortune Hunters*. It's about people who search for lost treasures, like divers who try to find the wrecks of old ships that went down with holds full of gems and gold coins. A nonfiction account, just like his book on old Centerlight would be.

Author: Tolenski, Peter C. $19.95. I click on MORE INFO and skip to the end of the book—the author photo on the last page. He's a little bit younger, beardless, with thin, dark hair—he hadn't started shaving his head yet. But there's no question it's the same guy.

I feel myself deflating like a balloon. I was so sure I was on to something. But Mr. Tolenski turns out to be 100 percent legit.

I'm back to square one.

At school that week, there's a surprise lockdown drill. I end up barricaded in the supply closet of the art room with Ronnie and Joey.

Almost immediately, I feel the shelves of paints and construction paper closing in on me. The weeks I spent lying in the backyard weren't fun, but at least I was out in the open.

"Wouldn't you know it?" I complain. "Why do they have to call this now, when we're stuck in a shoebox?"

"Are you kidding, sweetie?" Ronnie crows. "This is the best place in the whole building! What, you'd rather be in the locker room smelling sweat socks for the next hour?"

"What's so great about a closet?" I demand.

Joey is already patting a gigantic clay mustache onto his upper lip. "I've always wanted one of these. How do I look?"

"Slightly uglier than usual," Ronnie decides. "But with the beard—"

He grabs a fistful of clay and tries to smear it onto his friend's jawline. But Joey ducks and the gigantic dollop ends up oozing down the side of his face.

"Yay—sideburns!" Ronnie cheers.

Joey grabs him in a headlock and smashes his face into a plastic tray of Sharpies. Colored pens spill out, raining down on Ronnie.

There's a sharp rap at the door. "Keep it down in there!" comes the voice of the art teacher. "You're supposed to be silent!"

"Can't hear you, Miss Quinn," Joey calls back. "We're in the closet!"

He and Ronnie both crack up at this.

"Shhh!" I hiss. "She's going to hang us by our thumbs!"

"She can't open the door," Ronnie reasons, still in the headlock. "Not in lockdown drill." His flailing hand clamps on to an open package of pipe cleaners. He dumps it over Joey's head and continues to pummel him with the empty box.

In reply, Joey picks one of the fallen markers up off the floor, uncaps it, and waves it under Ronnie's nose. "Take a sniff!"

It gets a scream from Ronnie. "Cut it out! Get it away! That stuff stinks!"

Joey cackles diabolically. "Smell me!" he commands in a booming voice. "I smell beautiful!"

Ronnie grabs a tube of green oil paint and squeezes out a blob that hits Joey full in the face.

"Hey!" Joey lets go just long enough for Ronnie to get free and tackle him to the floor.

Playing peacemaker, I get down there and pull them apart. The next thing I know, *I'm* the one in Joey's headlock, and Ronnie is waving the marker under *my* nose.

"Smell me!"

So help me, it really is the stinkiest marker ever manufactured—like a combination of turpentine and sewer gas.

"Hey, stop it!" I sputter.

Now they're both chanting "Smell me!" and laughing like crazy.

"Come on, you guys! You know I have trouble breathing!"

At that moment, the all-clear bell sounds. The drill is over.

The door flies open and a furious Miss Quinn takes in the wreckage of her supply closet. Joey has green paint on his face, a clay beard and mustache, and multi-colored pipe cleaners in his hair—and a lot of that stuff has been transferred to Ronnie, me, and the floor in the course of the struggle. Construction paper, markers, and paintbrushes are everywhere. If looks could kill, we'd all be dead—which is really unfair, because none of this is my fault.

"The three of you are going to Mr. Federle's office," the art teacher snarls, "but not until this closet is exactly the way it was before." And she closes us in again.

I pick up a handful of fallen markers and dump them back in the tray. I'm bending down for another load when I realize I'm the only one cleaning. Ronnie and Joey are watching me, their expressions serious and unreadable.

"Whatever you do, don't help me," I say sarcastically.

Ronnie rakes me with suspicious eyes. "What's with you, sweetie? I thought that breathing stuff was all cured."

"It is—mostly," I reply. "But when you practically shove that marker up my nose—"

"That doesn't explain everything, man," Joey grumbles. "Like when you blew off Splat Night—how does TB fit into that?"

"It's like you're never down to hang with us anymore," Ronnie puts in.

"That's not it," I protest. But the truth is they're right. I don't hang out with them—or any of my school friends—as much as I used to. It's nothing against them. These days, the investigation is taking up every minute of my spare time.

"There's something up with you, sweetie," Ronnie insists. "Like why did you call my dad at his office to ask about that hole in our fence? You knew exactly what happened. It was your stupid friend Zoo-doo's stupid dead dog."

"That's not her name," I say sharply. "And she's not my friend either. She won't even talk to me anymore."

"So what does that have to do with my dad?" he

demands. "Did you think I was lying? Were you checking up on me? What do you care about our fence?"

I feel guilty keeping it from Ronnie that I suspect his dad. But I'll never be able to forget how Mr. Lindahl went ballistic that day. Anybody who could get that mad at his own son might be capable of anything.

I'm torn. Ronnie and Joey took me under their wing when I didn't know a soul at Centerlight Middle School. They deserve an explanation. But I can't tell them about the investigation, and not just because Ronnie's father is a suspect. Those guys think ZeeBee's crazy. And the fact that she believes her dog was murdered is the craziest thing about her.

I'm caught in the middle between ZeeBee and my friends. ZeeBee already hates me. If Ronnie and Joey turn on me too, I'll be totally alone.

21

Zarabeth

I'm not spying on Keenan anymore.

Oh, I still think he's plotting against me. But I have a new attitude: Who cares?

It bugs me a little that someone with a grudge against our family has gotten hold of Wayne's bike and won't give it back. Even more annoying, Dad (who's technically an officer of the law and should uphold justice) won't let me go over to Keenan's and re-steal it. I even called Wayne in Toronto to complain about the unfairness of it, but it doesn't bother him at all. He's got almost enough money saved up for a car. His exact words were "Let him keep it." Like a bike is no different than a hockey card or a stick of gum, or something cheap like that.

Whatever. If it doesn't bother Wayne, why should it bother me? I'm moving on. I've moved on already. Keenan? Keenan who?

I'm living a Keenan-free life. When I'm standing in line at the fro-yo shop my mind doesn't linger on all the times Keenan and I came here together. My only concern is what toppings I want—that and to stay away from the rum raisin. You might guess that the onetime rum-running capital of the world could make decent rum raisin frozen yogurt. But you'd be wrong.

"*Zarabeth*," comes an oily voice from ahead of me.

The last person I'm in the mood to deal with. "How's it going, Ronnie?"

"It's going fine," he tells me, "but I hear you and your *boyfriend* are on the outs."

"I don't have a boyfriend."

"Well, not *now*," he reasons. "You broke up."

"Not now, not ever," I insist. "You're the one with the bromance with Keenan."

He shakes his head. "That guy's too weird. Tuber-culosis. Ooh—don't touch me. I'm breathing."

"It's a real thing, you know," I snap back. Why am I defending Keenan? Keenan who? "It's a dangerous disease. People die from it."

"He got better a long time ago," Ronnie argues. "It wasn't any *disease* that made him call my dad and talk his ear off about the hole in our fence."

I'm instantly alert. I know all about the hole in the Lindahls' fence, which came courtesy of Barney. The *real* Barney—I glance outside, where Barney Two is tied up, waiting for me. This pretender couldn't put a hole in a fence made of tracing paper.

"My family paid to have that fixed," I say angrily. "The fact that your dad didn't get the work done isn't our fault. What does it have to do with Keenan?"

"I should be asking *you* that," he retorts. "Why is Keenan asking nosy questions about a mutt he never laid eyes on—who was dead before he even set foot on the island? I'm not an idiot, Zarabeth. *You're* the only connection."

I start to retort but my tongue freezes. Ronnie's right. I'm the only link between Keenan and the Lindahls' fence. Keenan wouldn't have known about Barney if I hadn't told him.

What does Keenan care about a broken fence . . . ?

It hits me: He talked with Mr. Lindahl, just like he talked with Michael Farnsworth, the Piccolis, the Quayle sisters, Martin Stickle, the Chaikens, and Leon Ping—all people who had run-ins with Barney. He's plotting against me, reaching out to everybody who has a grudge against my family. But one thing about this "plot" doesn't make sense: What's it for? Are they going to form a club to complain about a dog who's been gone for more than six months? Host potluck suppers to assassinate our character and call us names? What would be the point? It's not like Centrelight is one of those TV islands where your neighbors can vote you off.

So why would Keenan Cardinal talk to a group of random adults who have nothing in common except for the fact that they're all Barney-haters?

Keenan's words come back to me: *I believe you that Barney was murdered.*

Ronnie reaches the front of the line and turns away to place his order. That's a good thing, because I'm pretty sure I've gone white to the ears.

I believe you that Barney was murdered . . .

And now Keenan is talking to Barney's worst enemies—the people who stood to gain the most from

Barney being out of the picture . . .

It's my turn to order, but I'm frozen with shock. I don't want yogurt; I want *Keenan*. I have to tell him that I understand. Maybe even (I never do this, but it might be unavoidable) apologize.

"Hey—" Ronnie's holding his sundae, peering at me in what almost looks like concern. "You okay?"

"I—I—" Sentence unfinished, I wheel on him and run out of there, leaping on my bike and pedaling hard for Keenan's house. I'm halfway down the block before a distant yapping reminds me to go back and untie the leash so Barney Two can run along behind me.

I get to Keenan's and toss my bike, wheels spinning, on the front lawn. Yet as I stride onto the porch and reach for the doorbell, I lose my nerve.

What if I'm wrong? I don't think I am, but still. If he's plotting against me, then I'm playing right into his hands.

And if I'm wrong about being wrong, that's almost worse. It means I've been giving Keenan the silent treatment when he's believed me all this time. More than that—he's taken it a step further and is actually trying to find out who killed Barney.

Keenan's the best friend I ever had and I treated him like toenail fungus!

Three centimeters short of the doorbell, my finger stops in midair. What if he won't talk to me? Nobody could blame him. I made an idiot out of myself, but that's not as bad as how unfair I've been. He was on my side and I spit in his face.

I make a U-turn on the porch and march straight back to my bike. Barney Two looks up at me, head cocked in tail-wagging confusion.

"Saddle up, buster," I tell him through clenched teeth. "We're leaving."

Then that dumb dog does something so unexpected, so annoying, that I almost can't believe it. He runs right to the house, plants himself beneath a second-story window, and starts barking his ridiculous little head off.

"Cut it out!" I hiss. "He'll hear you."

Too late. A tall, slim figure appears in the window. Keenan. I can't actually see it, but I *know* that eyebrow of his is up. The mere thought of it makes me crazy.

I duck behind a bush. That's all I need to make my humiliation complete: to be caught skulking around his house.

A minute later, the front door opens and Keenan is kneeling on the grass, scratching the overgrown chipmunk behind his floppy ears. "What are you

doing here, Barney Two? Good to see you, buddy."
It's almost a joyous reunion. Keenan always did like
that dog way too much—another one of his annoying
qualities.

Finally, he stands up and announces, "You can come
out now, ZeeBee. I know you're here. Barney Two
never goes anywhere without you."

I emerge slowly, wishing I could just die and blow
away.

"Keenan," I begin. "I came to say— What I have to
tell you is—"

"Me first, ZeeBee," he interrupts. "There's something you need to see."

"What?" I ask.

He shakes his head. "I can't describe it. You have to
see for yourself."

I wait while he gets Wayne's bike, then follow him
through the streets, Barney Two trotting along with
us. We cross over to the Canadian side, and I note that
we're getting closer to home.

"My house?" I query when we turn onto my block.

"Close by" is his reply.

We pass home and continue beyond the community
hall to the cul-de-sac. Keenan gets off his bike and
starts down a footpath into the woods.

I'm confused. "Where are we going?"

He just keeps walking. Barney Two and I have to scramble to keep up. After a couple of minutes, he stops so suddenly that I bump into him from behind.

"We're here," he says.

"We're where?" We've come to a small clearing, but so what? The only difference is in Barney Two. Something's bugging him. He hangs back, whining.

That's when it hits me. The clearing is full of small animals—*dead* animals, scattered like the wind blew them here. That's why it took so long to notice them. Not a single one is moving.

Horrified, I look at Keenan. "What happened here?"

In answer, he reaches for two fallen sticks and, working them like pincers, picks up a flat gray object on the ground. It's shriveled and dry, covered in dirt, and a couple of ants cling to it. But the texture looks kind of familiar. Almost like—

"Is that—*meat*?"

He nods soberly. "All these animals ate it, and that's why they died. It was poisoned."

I'm still clueless. "But how did it get here?"

"I think Barney brought it here."

"*My* Barney?"

"You were right all along, ZeeBee," he says grimly.

"Barney was murdered. Someone fed him a poisoned steak . . ."

He says more, but I don't hear any of it because of the roaring in my ears. Suddenly, everything becomes so clear. If someone gave Barney a steak, of course he would have brought it to a secluded place like this. (Barney never shared.) But partway through the meal, he would have started to feel sick and abandoned the meat to all these poor animals and birds who went on to share his feast and his fate.

The rest of it I remember all too well. Barney wasn't himself that night. I should have known when we got a delivery and he didn't even try to chase the UPS guy. But I didn't see it. And in the morning—

"ZeeBee—"

The next thing I know, Keenan is standing beside me, awkwardly patting my shoulder, which is bizarre until I realize that tears are streaming down my cheeks. This is even more awful than it sounds, because it violates my strict No Crying policy.

"I knew it!" I choke. "I knew it!" Yet as soon as the words are out of my mouth, I realize that I *didn't* know—at least not definitely. Now, seeing that it's 100 percent true is like losing my dog all over again.

Someone killed Barney—not in my imagination, but in cold, cruel reality.

"You did know," Keenan agrees in a gentle voice. "I should have believed you. I'm sorry."

I'm about to apologize back when Barney Two inches forward and starts nosing around the poisoned meat, which is on the ground where Keenan dropped the two sticks.

"No!" I fling myself to the forest floor and snatch away that cocker gerbil a split second before he can take a bite and get himself killed.

Keenan grabs the meat and holds it high in the air.

"Get rid of it," I tell him, my voice cracking. "Bury it before it poisons anybody else."

"I can't," he replies.

"Why not?"

"It's evidence!"

Evidence. The word clicks into place.

I wasn't wrong about Keenan! *That*'s what he's been doing these past weeks.

Investigating Barney's murder.

22

Keenan

Three months ago, my home was a twelve-hundred-square-foot apartment on the thirty-second floor of a building in Shanghai, China, and tuberculosis was nothing more than a word I'd never heard before. Now I'm a survivor of it, sitting on the border between two countries on the opposite side of the world, with a bag of poison in my bedroom.

It's just the dried-up meat, but there's still poison in there—enough to kill plenty of small animals and birds in the woods beyond ZeeBee's house. Yes, the evidence lives with me, sealed inside a Ziploc sandwich bag hidden at the bottom of my sock drawer, so the cleaning lady won't find it.

My room has become investigation headquarters. Photographs of the suspects peer down from my wall. ZeeBee calls them the Notorious Nine—although there are really eleven of them, since the Piccolis and Quayle sisters are double suspects. We get the pictures from Facebook pages, Instagram feeds, and other internet sources—an online ad for Mr. Chaiken's store; Ms. Batista's bio on the opera company's site; Mr. Tolenski's author webpage; a profile of the Quayle sisters from the Canadian Horticultural Society. At the very top, ZeeBee tapes up a picture of the late Barney with the caption *R.I.P.*

"For motivation," she explains.

To be honest, I'm not too thrilled about that part. It's a little creepy going to sleep every night with a dead dog standing guard over my bed. But it's great that ZeeBee and I aren't enemies anymore, and I'm thrilled to have a partner. Plus—no offense to ZeeBee—having Barney Two back in my life might be even better. The investigation has fetch breaks now. When our heads are pounding from hours and hours of staring at evidence in the hope of noticing something we missed before, we can go downstairs and throw a ball around. I'm really starting to gain the spaniel's trust, even if he does look over at ZeeBee every couple of minutes to confirm that it's okay to play with me. He's almost as loyal to her as she is indifferent to him.

As for ZeeBee, the simple fact is that two heads are better than one. When we start bouncing ideas off each other, we come up with things we never would have thought of individually. Already we have notes up on the wall under every suspect—anything that might be even remotely connected to Barney's poisoning.

For example, Elspeth and Muriel Quayle have exhibited at the Toronto International Flower Show every year since 1966—*until last season*. Why did they stop? Their greenhouse was smashed by a "horrid canine individual," so there was no way to have spring flowers ready in time for the March event. Less than a month later, Barney was dead.

Martin Stickle's Instagram account has pictures from every bike rally he races in. But in only one does he appear with a bandage on his right hand. The date: April 20—two days after ZeeBee found Barney's body. Did that bandage cover a burn that came from contact with a powerful poison?

Why was the Oakland County Opera Company's performance of *Madame Butterfly* canceled on April 18? Could it have been that the star—Arabella Batista—was too upset to perform, because of the terrible thing she had done the night before?

ZeeBee and I believe that the April 17 meeting at the community hall holds the key to cracking the case. That evening, all of our Notorious Nine spent three hours practically across the street from the murder victim.

It's ZeeBee who remembers that the community foundation videotapes their meetings and posts them online. We settle ourselves in front of my computer to watch.

"The camera's pointed at the podium, not the seats," ZeeBee observes with a frown. "How are we supposed to see who's there?"

"Let's give it some time," I advise.

It doesn't take long before I wish I'd never said that. If reading about the meeting is boring, actually watching it happen is boring to the fiftieth power. There are six thousand people on Centerlight, and every single one—American or Canadian—has a different opinion about fixing up the lighthouse, and who should have to pay for it.

I'm aware of a faint rumbling sound to my left. ZeeBee has dozed off and is snoring softly into my ear. Even Barney Two is curled up at her feet, eyelids drooping.

"Hey—" I shake her by the shoulder. "It's your town. It's your dog. If I have to watch it, so do you."

"At least put it on fast-forward," she pleads. "On the off chance that something important happens, we can slow it down."

Good idea. It's still boring, but at least we're plowing through it faster—and we don't have to listen to it.

Then something *does* happen. As the meeting races on, people begin to come into view on the right side of the screen. They blur past the podium and disappear out of the frame only to return a little later.

ZeeBee frowns. "What's that?"

I back up the recording and play it at normal speed. What we're actually seeing is attendees leaving and reentering the meeting room.

"The door must be near the front," I conclude. "So every time somebody goes to the bathroom, they pass through camera range."

"Oh goody," ZeeBee yawns. "I always wanted to know the bathroom habits of my neighbors."

But I'm excited. "Don't you get it? Our suspects are in that room. And if any of them leave, we'll be able to track how long they're gone. Anything longer than a few minutes is plenty of time to run across the street and plant that poisoned meat for Barney."

The first suspect to appear is Mr. Ping, and he's carrying a satchel just the right size for a steak.

"I'll bet it's him," ZeeBee says darkly. "I don't trust cat owners. And Fagan is a saber-toothed tiger disguised as a house pet."

I shoot her a cockeyed glance. It's not what you'd expect to hear from the owner of a dog that used to be the scourge of two countries.

Using the stopwatch on my phone, I time Mr. Ping's absence. Three minutes and eleven seconds.

"What do you think?" ZeeBee asks eagerly. "Is that long enough to go out and—commit the crime?"

"Depends," I reply. "How long does it take to get out of the building and cross the street to your house?"

She's still pondering this when Muriel Quayle appears on the screen, carrying a purse that could easily hide the murder weapon. I start the timer.

We focus on the screen as the elder of the two sisters

finds herself hemmed in by a stray chair and hurls it out of her path as easily as swatting a fly.

"Yikes," ZeeBee comments. "I always thought of the Quayles as frail old ladies, but remind me never to get in their way."

It seems like she's gone forever. I keep my eye on the stopwatch on my phone. "Five twenty-seven," I report, when she finally returns. "That's more than enough time."

ZeeBee's skeptical. "Girls take longer in the bathroom. And don't forget she's slower than Mr. Ping because she's old."

"That didn't stop her from tossing a steel chair around," I point out. "And you should have seen the look on their faces when she talked about what Barney did to their greenhouse."

We keep watching. Mr. Farnsworth is next, but he's back in two minutes flat. Ms. Batista goes twice—for 4:03 and 3:37—but ZeeBee reminds me that opera singers have to drink a lot of water to keep their throats clear. Ronnie's dad is up shortly after that. He has no bag, but he could have easily stashed the meat somewhere to pick it up and do the evil deed.

As the video continues, every single one of the

Notorious Nine marches past the camera, with the exception of Mr. Tolenski.

"The guy must have a bladder like a king-size waterbed," ZeeBee mutters.

"Either that or they bored him into unconsciousness," I add.

There's one point near the end of the tape where you can actually hear distant barking, and I know it has to be Barney. Who else would be loud enough to saturate the neighborhood, penetrate the building, float upstairs into a closed meeting room, and still have the volume to make it onto the tape?

ZeeBee is biting her lip, so I know that she hears it too. No wonder she's sad. To her, this must be nothing less than a voice from beyond the grave.

When we've watched the whole thing—all two hours and forty-seven minutes—we make a chart of the suspects and the length of their bathroom breaks:

L. Ping–3:11

M. Quayle–5:27

M. Farnsworth–1:58

A. Batista–4:03, 3:37

D. Lindahl–3:46

Our next stop is the community hall. ZeeBee and I sit in the gallery and actually time each other going downstairs, out of the building, and across the street to toss a steak over the Tices' fence. Obviously, we don't have any meat, so we use a hockey puck. During ZeeBee's turn, Barney Two runs along with her. He even dashes in through the gate and fetches the puck. It's still in his mouth when the two of them burst back into the meeting room. He drops it at her feet, panting excitedly in anticipation of the next round.

She glares down at him. "What are you so amped up about? You think this is a game?"

I stick up for Barney Two. "He's a dog. What do you expect him to think? If you tried playing with him once in a while, he might not go ape over a hockey puck."

She makes a face. "Who wants to play with *him*?"

I just shake my head at her.

We compare our times: ZeeBee gets the job done in 3:25. I'm seven seconds slower—3:32.

"Anyone who took that long or more could have poisoned Barney," I conclude.

We check the chart. We can rule out Ping, Farnsworth, Stickle, and Tolenski, but not Lola Piccoli. Even though she was absent less than 3:30, she could still have been in cahoots with her husband, who took longer.

My eyes meet ZeeBee's. The Quayle sisters, Arabella Batista, Mr. Lindahl, the Piccolis, and Mr. Chaiken are still suspects.

23

Zarabeth

My parents are treating Keenan like a long-lost son returning after a painful absence. It's really annoying.

Don't get me wrong. I'm thrilled that Keenan and I are friends again, and I'm grateful for all the detective work he's done trying to find out who poisoned Barney. Still, it's pretty obvious that the reason Mum and Dad are falling all over themselves to be nice to Keenan is that they think I was wrong to be so hard on him. Okay, I *was* wrong—I'm the first to admit it. But they didn't know that at the time. They should have sided with their own daughter over some random guy who doesn't even live in the same country.

Or maybe they just love Keenan because he keeps me out of their hair, which is even worse. Whatever the reason, he's now the prince of Tommy-Gun Ferguson's former residence. Me? I just live here.

Whenever Keenan comes over, my parents break their necks to make him feel welcome. Dad grills his favorite Canadian food—back bacon on a bun. They're buddies now. They reminisce about the good old days when Dad arrested him over by the lighthouse.

"Yeah, real funny," I growl. "Like Canada needs to send a trained border officer to pick up some loser passed out in the tall grass."

"Well, he wasn't passed out until I started chasing him," Dad chuckles. To Keenan he adds, "You were kicking dirt in my face for a while there."

The two of them laugh like nothing has ever been so funny. They almost remind me of Ronnie and Joey, who could probably have a giggle-fit over bubonic plague. Maybe it's a guy thing. (You don't expect your dad to be a guy, though.)

In fairness to Mum and Dad, I have to admit that

Mr. Cardinal is really nice to me too. But that makes a lot more sense. Keenan was basically dying of TB when I came along. (Okay, maybe not dying, but he had to lie in the yard all day.) Plus nobody wants their kid to be friendless in a new town, so I'm the only option. When he tried being friends with the school crowd, he wound up unconscious and under arrest.

The one thing we don't tell any of our parents about is our ongoing investigation. Mine would freak out. They're patting themselves on the back because they think they've finally convinced me that Barney died of old age. And Keenan's dad? He might put two and two together and figure out all the pictures and notes on his son's wall. Right now he seems to believe it's some kind of school assignment. (Keenan has this theory that there's no limit to what you can get away with if adults think it's for your education. Must be an American thing. Canadians would never fall for it.) But once parents get suspicious, they're like bloodhounds. The last thing we need is Mr. Cardinal calling up *my* folks to talk about it.

Five suspects. Technically seven people, since there are two Piccolis and two Quayle sisters. No matter what we're doing, our minds are always on the case.

Not that it's doing us much good. The problem is we're investigating something that happened nearly six months ago, so the trail is pretty cold. It's not as if we can follow our suspects and catch them in the act. The act is long over. Don't I know it.

We keep digging. Keenan finds out on the internet that Mrs. Piccoli, now retired, has a PhD in chemistry. It would be easy for her to whip up a killer cocktail. But then we tour the Chaikens' grocery store and find no fewer than fourteen products that could be used as poison. And if the Chaikens can sell them, any of the others can buy them. So it's another dead end.

"You should get Ronnie talking about his father," I suggest to Keenan. "Maybe Mr. Lindahl got bitten as a child, and he hates all dogs."

We're sitting on my porch, splitting a takeout poutine. Keenan doesn't like the cheese curds (typical American) and is slipping them down to Barney Two. He thinks I don't notice. A border officer's daughter notices everything.

"That sounds like a stretch," Keenan tells me. "We can put everybody's life under a microscope and it still won't prove anything. We already know the suspects had a grudge against Barney. That's why they became suspects."

I glance up as the mail truck stops in front of our house and Mrs. Canmore, the letter carrier, starts up the walk. Instantly, Barney Two abandons his cheese curds and darts over to greet her, wagging and yipping. She reaches down to pet him and he licks her hand.

She smiles as she hands me the mail. "What a difference a few months make. I used to have to run for my life at this address. This little fellow is adorable."

She's right. Barney used to make her life miserable, barking the neighborhood down, and chasing her back and forth across the border. He wasn't any nicer to the American mail carriers on the Michigan side. He once chewed up one of those U.S. Post Office buggies like it was made of tissue paper. Dad had to jump through hoops to get him out of trouble. In both countries, it's a federal crime to interfere with the mail.

Still, it hurts that Mrs. Canmore prefers this little runt to big, beautiful Barney.

It must show on my face, because she softens. "Sorry, ZeeBee. We all know how fond you were of Barney."

"Thanks," I mumble. But when the truck moves on, I turn to Keenan. "What's the matter with us? Why isn't *she* on the suspect list?"

"She wasn't at the meeting," he reasons.

"How can we be so sure the killer was at the meeting? Mrs. Canmore could have been out here with that poisoned steak. Or the FedEx and UPS guys. What about the American mail carriers? They hated Barney even worse, because their trucks have open sides. They were sitting ducks."

He looks back at me helplessly. I have a terrible thought: What if, after all our hard work, we're no closer to the truth than we were before all this began?

"I hate this heap," I complain, hanging on to the rail. "Why couldn't we just take the Canada Customs boat?"

My parents and I are on the ferry, crossing the river, choking on the solid wall of diesel exhaust that gets blasted down to the passenger deck by the prevailing winds on the St. Clair. I'm used to it, but my poor mother is turning green.

"We can't, ZeeBee," Dad explains. "First of all, there's a crew using it now. And second, how would it look if I treat government property like our own personal pleasure craft while all the other families have to ride the ferry?"

"No one would even notice us," I insist. "We're the only people going to the middle school anyway. All the other kids my age on Centrelight go to the Michigan school—in case you forgot."

"We haven't forgotten," Mum assures me. "How could we forget? You remind us every twenty minutes."

"Anyway, you and Keenan are friends again, right?" Dad adds.

"Yeah," I agree, "but what does that have to do with the fact that I'm all alone at the school I have to go to?"

Mum sighs. "Whatever you do, don't admit that things ever go your way."

Obviously, the diesel fumes are making her grouchy.

At school, we hook up with Chloe and her family since we're in most of the same classes. The McFarlanes are nice, but they're not islanders, and it makes us different from each other in a way I'm not sure I totally understand. I love Centrelight, but it's kind of an unusual place to be from.

The teacher meetings go okay. There are a few left-handed compliments about my "flair for the dramatic," which is Canadian for I talk too much, get on people's nerves, and make a big stink over nothing. But my grades are solid, so I get away with it. Mum and Dad are happy, which is all I can ask for.

Pretty soon, we're back on the ferry, choking on fumes again. It's always a little longer heading west. The difference is only a minute and a half, but it bugs me. Also, Dad makes us walk home from the wharf, since he didn't want to use a government jeep.

The first sign that something's wrong comes as we step onto the front porch. The door is open a crack.

Frowning, Mum turns to Dad. "Did you forget to lock up?"

That's when we see the busted window of the side-light—like someone punched through the glass to be able to reach the latch inside.

A jolt of shock shakes me as the meaning of this sinks in. Our house has been broken into!

Cautiously, Dad eases the door wide.

"Shouldn't you—you know—call for backup?" I ask anxiously.

"Stay here," he orders, his voice quiet but firm. He steps inside, alert to any sound.

It takes him a few minutes to determine that there are no intruders inside our house—at least not any-more. But someone has been here.

"What happened in there?" my mother asks anx-iously.

I detect a subtle change in the look on my father's

face. He's no longer Dad; he's Officer Darryl Tice. He's thinking like a cop now.

"They tossed the place," he reports.

"Tossed?" I query.

I learn the meaning of the word pretty quickly. Every drawer in our house has been pulled out and dumped on the floor. Every cabinet and closet has been ransacked, their contents flung all over. Heart pounding, I run up to my room. It's a disaster area. My stuff is scattered across the floor. Barney Two is there, whining unhappily, wrapped up in his leash and knotted to the bedpost.

I quickly untie him. "Some watchdog you are," I growl at him.

He hangs his head in shame, almost as if he understands.

"Not only didn't you protect the house; you *let* them tie you up." I examine him closely for any possible injuries. Considering how trusting he is, the little doofus could have wound up hurt. Luckily, he seems healthy (and clueless) as ever.

"You're a disgrace to the Barney name," I mutter. "You could have at least bitten somebody."

He responds with wet kisses. Very annoying. But to be honest, I'm too upset to be really mad. Somebody

flowerbed! How come nobody ever listens to me?"

"ZeeBee," he says sternly, "this is not a game. A real crime has been committed, and we were the victims of it. I want you to leave the investigating to the professionals."

"But, Dad—"

"Zarabeth—"

I shut up. When he hits me with the full Zarabeth, I can be sure he means business.

It's just frustrating, because I'm right and he's wrong. And if all these other cops agree with him, they're wrong too. Seriously, if this has always been the level of police know-how on Centrelight, then it's no wonder people like Tommy-Gun Ferguson did so well here.

I retreat from the group and slip out the side door, that useless Barney Two sticking to me like glue. Oh sure, he was totally AWOL when burglars were ransacking our house, but now he's raring to go. What a hero. He probably thinks I'll protect him. Good luck with that.

I hesitate. *Do* we need protection? What if the intruders are still in the neighborhood? I glance around. There's a glow in the sky over our house created by so many flashers. About ten police cars are parked on our street. Any lawbreaker with half a brain would have gotten himself miles from here by now. Come to think of it, this would be the perfect time to commit the crime of the century anywhere else on the island, because all the cops are right here. Not that any police officers on Centrelight can see what's happening right in front of their noses. If they could, they'd listen to me.

I square my shoulders and begin striding up the road toward the border, Barney Two scrambling to keep pace. There's one person on this island who will take me seriously on this—the guy who was on my side even when I was treating him like pond scum.

I'm going to see Keenan.

24

Keenan

When my computer goes into screen-saver mode, it starts to scroll through all the pictures I have saved on it. I never set it to do that. It's been happening on its own ever since the last software update. Go figure.

My homework done, I lean back in my chair and watch the images marching across the screen. There's one of Mom, Klaus, and me, with two giraffes standing in the background like it's the most normal thing in the world. It's from the safari we went on during our stint in Lesotho. I can see my swollen glands, and I think back to all those ear infections—Mom didn't want to have my tonsils out until we were back in the States at Christmas. It was a pretty lousy Christmas, too, with all that ice cream bubbling out my nose.

I spent a few days with Dad that holiday, and I know we were in Centerlight—but that's about all I remember, except how cold it was. We were stuck in the house most of the time, because of a twenty-two-inch snowfall. We had mac and cheese for Christmas dinner, and I thought that was pretty awesome.

That was four days. Now I've been here four months, yet I feel like I've been in Centerlight forever. Maybe it's the *smallness* that does it to you. Life with Mom and Klaus was fun, living in gigantic, exotic cities. But those places have so much going on that you can't focus on any one thing for very long. And just when you're starting to really notice what's there, it's time to move on.

Here it's totally different. There are two riverbanks, a lighthouse, and, cutting through everything, the border. It should be boring; it *is* boring, in a way. But it's familiar and reassuring too.

It's almost as if I was just a spectator before, and my

life was this cool theme park I got to visit. It took what happened to a dog I never laid eyes on to show me what's real. Okay, even I have to admit the original Barney sounds pretty awful. But that doesn't give anybody the right to poison him. Someone did that—someone I pass on the street every day, who cuts the grass, and buys groceries, and carries an umbrella when it's raining. That person is out there, getting away with it, scot-free. I don't know what kind of punishment to expect for this kind of thing. It's not legal murder—but there should be something. Jail time. A big fine. A million hours of community service. Even a Twitter hashtag about what a lowlife you are, so your neighbors will know what you did. Something!

The injustice of it is making me nuts. It's the first thing I think of when I wake up in the morning, and I'm still mentally leafing through the suspect list when I close my eyes at night. This is not the person I was four months ago in Shanghai. This isn't the kind of thing I'd even notice back then. Sure, I saw a lot of stuff that would look cool on Instagram. But seeing isn't the same as getting involved. As sick as I was, I feel more alive now than ever before.

There's a loud crack, and the whole house seems to jump.

"Keenan?" my dad calls from downstairs. "Everything okay?"

"Fine," I confirm. "I think a bat might have flown into the side of the house." In Asia, there are these big bats called flying foxes that can shake up a whole apartment building if they run into one by mistake.

I go to the window. Nothing broken. Then I peer down and spot ZeeBee. She's already got another big rock in her hand, and this one's bound to shatter the glass.

I heave up the sash and rasp, "Don't throw that!"

"Keenan, it's me," she whispers.

"I know it's you," I reply. "Why can't you ring the doorbell like normal people?"

"It's late. I didn't want to disturb your dad."

"He'd probably notice a giant hunk of concrete knocking the house over." I figured that would get at least a smile out of her, but she seems really distracted. "I'll be right down," I promise.

By the time I come out into the yard, she's sitting on the grass with her back against a tree, Barney Two standing guard like a sentry.

"What's the big emergency?" I ask.

"Our house got broken into tonight."

At first, I think she's making a big deal out of

nothing, like the voices in the night she considers proof that Centerlight's gangster past isn't over yet. But as she describes the emptied drawers, ransacked cabinets, and overturned furniture that greeted the family when they returned from ZeeBee's school, it sinks in that this is all too real. Centerlight is such a quiet, sleepy place that it's hard to picture a robbery happening here.

"It wasn't a robbery," ZeeBee informs me. "Nothing was stolen. Not even a toothpick."

I'm confused. "Why would somebody break in to steal nothing?"

Her eyes flash in anger. "Why don't you come over and say that to the fifteen cops—including my own father—who don't know their butts from third base? Isn't it obvious? How many times have I told you the story of Tommy-Gun Ferguson's gold?"

"Yeah, but that's just a rumor—" She scowls at me, so I add, "And anyway, even if the gold exists, it isn't in your house, right?"

"I know that and you know that, but the burglars don't. What are we supposed to do? Put a sign on our house that says 'ATTENTION CROOKS: NO GOLD HERE'?"

I don't answer. ZeeBee's my friend—my best friend.

But when she talks about Prohibition and stashes of gold, I kind of tune her out. I can't help wondering if her problems with Ronnie and the crowd at Centerlight Middle have less to do with where she goes to school than the fact that she won't let this gangster stuff die. Someday I might even work up the courage to tell her so.

Okay, delete that. I never will.

I reach down and scratch Barney Two behind the ears. "This little guy seems okay. Was he in the house when it happened?"

She looks disgusted. "He sure was. He cooperated fully with the burglars. Some watchdog. If you look up *useless* in the dictionary, there's probably a picture of him." Her expression hardens. "If this had happened last year, things would have been pretty different, let me tell you."

"How?" I ask.

"Because it would have been *my* Barney instead of this wimp. And we would need a special cleanup crew to shampoo the shredded burglar out of the upholstery. These crooks will never know how lucky they are."

"Lucky," I echo vaguely. I'm reaching for something, but I can't put my finger on it. And in a flash, there it is, like the one piece of the jigsaw puzzle that brings all the different parts together into one clear image. "ZeeBee, what if the burglars weren't lucky at all? What if they made their own luck?"

"What are you talking about?" she mutters. "They still would have broken in, and this naked mole rat still would have let them."

"Look at the big picture," I insist. "All the time we've been investigating Barney's murder, we assumed he was poisoned by somebody who hated him. But what if the killer wasn't after revenge? What if he was after Tommy-Gun Ferguson's gold? Remember what the letter carrier said? She couldn't get near your house when Barney was alive. Well, the killer might have come to the same conclusion—that the only way to gain access to your house was to get rid of Barney."

It takes a moment for this to sink in. "You mean," ZeeBee barely whispers, "Barney was poisoned—for gold?"

She sounds so devastated that I almost say forget it, I've got it wrong. For ZeeBee, the subject of what happened to her dog is so painful that every new piece of information makes her relive the whole terrible experience—like picking off a scab too soon so the wound reopens and starts bleeding again.

On the other hand, how can I hide this from her? This is about more than just Barney. It's about the break-in at her house. The footprints and voices. Half of Centerlight considers ZeeBee a drama queen and a crank—including her own parents. This would prove that what she's been talking about all this time isn't just in her head. Somebody really has been after Tommy-Gun's gold.

"It's the only explanation," I say finally.

She looks stricken. "But our suspects—they're Barney-haters, not treasure hunters!"

I nod soberly. "We had it wrong from the start, so our suspect list is probably wrong too. That's not definite either. You can have a grudge against a dog and still be a greedy slimeball. But we have to figure your burglar and Barney's killer are the same person. Why else would anybody break in and steal *nothing*, not even cash and jewelry? And why your house out of every house on the island?"

She's bitter. "Then Barney was poisoned for nothing, because there wasn't any gold, or treasure, or secret stash."

"Are you sure?" I probe. "You know somebody tore up your house. How do you know he didn't find what he was looking for?"

"If there was any gold in that house," she replies, "I would have found it first. I've been searching since I was seven—ever since my dad stumbled on the hidey-hole in the basement. I've even drilled into walls so I could shine a flashlight on what's inside. Believe me, my parents really enjoyed that."

I nod reluctantly. It's logical that a smart crook like Tommy-Gun wouldn't stash his loot in the very first place the cops would look for it. He had Eliot Ness on his tail, one of the greatest lawmen in history.

My mind is racing so fast that my thoughts are spilling out my mouth before I even have a chance to figure out what they mean. "What about something else, then? Something that tells you where to *find* the gold. A clue. A map."

She shrugs. "There's the old map from the 1880s, but that was made a long time before Prohibition, when all the gangsters came to Centerlight."

"Instructions, then," I persist. "You know, 'forty paces to the west, sixty paces to the north.' But probably in some kind of code. You could have seen it a thousand times without realizing what it was."

ZeeBee's phone rings. "Uh-oh, my father. Probably not the best night to disappear." She answers the call. "Hi, Dad. I'm at Keenan's . . . Yeah, sorry to run out on you. I was 'leaving it to the professionals' . . . All right, I'll be home in a few minutes." She hangs up. "He sounds worried. I might be kind of in trouble."

"Tell your folks if there's anything I can do, they should just let me know."

"I volunteered you already," she informs me. "You're coming over tomorrow to help with the big cleanup. Be there by ten. Nine thirty would be better."

25

Zarabeth

By the time Keenan shows up on Saturday morning, the cleaning operation is well under way, and six heavy-duty trash bags are already out by the curb.

"It's my mother," I explain when his telltale eyebrow rises halfway up his forehead. "She's been waiting for an opportunity to get rid of our old junk for years."

He looks nervous. "I hope she's not getting rid of . . . too much junk."

I get his meaning. That's the real reason Keenan is here this morning, and it has very little to do with cleaning. Having your house get trashed isn't fun, but it has one side benefit: You have the chance to examine every single solitary inch of the place, including stuff that's been buried in drawers and lost in the depths of closets for years. If Tommy-Gun Ferguson left behind any hint about where he stashed his fortune, it's bound to pass through our hands at some point.

As we enter, Keenan pauses at the old map hanging in the living room. It got knocked off the wall during the break-in last night, so the glass is cracked. But otherwise, it's okay.

"I already checked," I whisper to him. "There are no secret markings, no X marks the spot. I even shone a black light on it after my parents went to bed last night. Nothing."

Dad pokes his head into the room. "Morning, Keenan. Appreciate your help. Word of advice—stay away from my wife or you'll end up in a garbage bag out by the curb. She's on a bit of a tear." He disappears down the basement stairs.

"He's right," I tell Keenan. "We'd better get going while there's still something left to search."

"Where do we start?" he asks.

"The cupola," I decide. "From there we'll work our way down."

The only piece of "furniture" up there is the bean-bag chair I sit on while I do my homework. It's been sliced open and the stuffing is all over the floor.

"This is the one part of the house Tommy-Gun built himself," I inform him. "But there's no place to hide anything."

Keenan turns on his cellphone flashlight and begins examining the rounded ceiling. "Check for any letters, numbers, or symbols scratched into the wood."

It takes some doing because we're craning our necks. But after a few minutes, we conclude that nothing's there. We cram the remains of the chair into a lawn bag and head downstairs to the bedrooms. Mum is delighted. She takes our bag and adds it to three more at the top of the stairs, waiting to be taken outside—used clothing for Goodwill.

We go to my room next. I can tell Keenan's a little shocked by the condition of the place. The dresser drawers and the contents of the closet have been dumped on the floor. I had to dig myself a path to my bed last night so I could sleep. All my stuff—schoolbooks, papers, board games, toys from when I was younger—is scattered around.

I answer his unasked question. "There's no 'neatness counts' for the kind of person who's rotten enough to poison a dog."

"Yeah, but where do we even start to look for clues in all this?"

"You take the closet," I decide. "I'll handle my own underwear, thank you very much."

The actual cleanup takes maybe twenty minutes. The hard part is searching for something that might be coded instructions or directions. Face it, we have no idea what we might be looking for. We can only hope that we'll recognize it if we see it. The one thing we know for sure is it has to be something that was in the house eighty-plus years ago when Tommy-Gun was choosing a place to hide his ill-gotten gains. That eliminates all our furniture and everything we brought to the house when we moved in, or purchased since.

Keenan discovers a series of notches carved into a doorframe in the hall, and we get really excited. Each marking has a notation beside it, letters and numbers. I grab a yardstick, and we measure the distance between the indentations, racking our brains for a relationship between them and the tiny pencil notes beside them. None of it makes any sense.

"Isn't that cute," my mother remarks over my shoulder. "You found the spot where Dad marked all your growth spurts on your birthdays, you and Wayne."

I feel like an idiot. That explains all the Zs and Ws. To make it worse, Keenan is smirking at me.

We scour Wayne's room and the guest room without any luck. Mum and Dad break for lunch, so we give the master a quick once-over. Nothing—at least nothing we can see.

The basement is the biggest mess of all, because it's where most of the junk of the house eventually winds up. Everything that we don't need but can't bring ourselves to throw out finds its way down there. Picture all that tossed in the middle of a dingy room: papers, tools and hardware, baby furniture, small appliances that don't work anymore, old mail, paint cans and brushes, extra tiles from long-forgotten repair jobs, books, school projects from Wayne and me—the list goes on and on. Add to that broken hunks of baseboard and wall plaster ripped down by our destructive visitor.

It's an endless, thankless marathon. The only good thing is that it proves that Keenan is a real friend. For sure nobody else would be standing here by my side, buried in random stuff and choking on plaster dust.

Even Barney Two can't stand it. He gives a couple of sneezes and escapes up the stairs. Coward! Although I have to admit that the original Barney had no patience for dust either (unless he was the one kicking it up).

Finally, Mum and Dad come down to relieve us. I note that my mother has brought a fresh box of green garbage bags. She's not thinking about Tommy-Gun's hidden fortune at all. Her business is cleanup, and business is booming.

My eyes meet Keenan's. He nods. We haven't gotten rid of anything, just organized the jumble into piles in the center of the floor. Our true goal is finding a clue to the whereabouts of the gold. And there's nothing down here.

Upstairs in the kitchen, we crack open a bag of chips and inhale it while Barney Two begs at my feet. Believe me, not a crumb escapes. This is the lunch we missed three hours ago, and we're both starving.

Keenan tries to sneak a chip under the table, but I snatch it out of his hand. "That little traitor deserted us in the basement. He's not getting anything here."

"Have a heart, ZeeBee," he argues. "Your folks are so wound up that I bet they forgot to feed him."

"Big deal," I snort. "They probably forgot to feed the real Barney too. And did he grovel pathetically?"

"No," he retorts. "He went after the Chaikens' cheese, or the Lindahls' steak, or the Quayles' flowers, or the interior of the Farnsworth Porsche."

I nod nostalgically. "He was so good at thinking out of the box."

I don't mean it as a joke, but Keenan laughs. And, yeah, it's pretty funny. I get that no matter what we're talking about, I'll always act like my Barney did it great, and Barney Two is a pale comparison. It almost makes me feel sorry for him. After all, it isn't Barney Two's fault that the original was a thousand times better than him.

I can laugh with Keenan now because we know that the bad things Barney did were not the reason he was poisoned. That's not to say people didn't really hate him—they did. But it isn't why he got murdered. And once I start laughing, I just can't stop. All the crazy mayhem Barney caused comes flooding back to me, and each incident is more hilarious than the last. I see the blizzard of earth hanging over the Piccolis' yard like a mushroom cloud as he buried the steak bones he stole from the Lindahls' barbecue. I see him descending upon Fagan like an avenging angel (an angel the size of a full-grown bull moose). I remember the trip over the bridge to bail him out of the dog pound in

St. Clair, Michigan—the look on his big homely face when he recognized us and realized he was saved. I hear the click of my dad's finger on the calculator as he added up all the money Barney had cost us in fines, replacing flowers and bushes, fixing downed and dug-up cable wires, paying doctor bills for people he'd plowed over, and reimbursing stores for ruined food and merchandise. Who knew there was a $250 penalty for when your dog pees in the eternal flame at the cemetery? I never would have if it wasn't for Barney. Dad said he was putting us in the poorhouse, and I felt bad, honest I did. But I felt pride too. Because deep in my heart, I knew nobody had a dog like mine.

I laugh until I'm choking on chips. Keenan has to pound me on the back, sending crumbs down to Barney Two on the floor. He laps them up grate-fully—Barney Two, not Keenan. (The real Barney never would have even noticed something so small.)

"Seriously, Keenan," I say when at last I get myself under control. "I know we're pretty much back to square one, but we've got to solve this somehow. It's the only way we'll ever get justice for Barney."

He looks thoughtful. "Maybe we're taking the wrong approach here. We'll drive ourselves nuts if we stare at every stain on the floor or scratch in the paint like it's a secret message from Tommy-Gun Ferguson. Wouldn't it be better if we try to see the big picture?"

I frown. "What big picture?"

"You're so used to this house that you probably don't notice how *different* it is," he explains. "Like the cupola up top. Or the stained-glass window in the living room. Or that fancy pattern inlaid into the border of the hardwood floor. Anything you have here but most houses don't could be a clue."

We get up and walk into the living room. Keenan's right. Our ceilings are fourteen feet high, and vaulted. Our fireplace is fieldstone, with a carved mantel. Parts of the wall are recessed for vases or artwork on pedestals. My mother likes to put plants in those niches, but Tommy-Gun was a lot richer than us, and probably had fancier taste. Could there have been another reason for those special features—a secret guide to hidden treasure?

"You know what always bugged me about your place?" Keenan says suddenly. "That carpet over there—the little one. Why do you need one square of carpet in the middle of the wood floor like that?"

I shrug. "The floors are wood and there are rugs on some of them. They came with the house. Mum says they're good quality, so we kept them."

He isn't sold. He kneels beside the carpet in question and points to a round spot, faded almost to white. "What's this?"

I point to the stained-glass window. "You see the clear center of that flower? There's a moment every afternoon where the sun shines through there and the beam gets focused on that place on the carpet. It's pretty cool. I used to watch for it when I was little. The exact timing must have been slightly different from day to day, depending on the position of the sun. But I always remember it happening pretty soon after I got home from school. Anyway, over the years, that dot on the rug got faded out."

"I'm not talking about the dot," Keenan tells me. "How come all the other carpets are positioned at random, but this one has its own special place sunken into the floor?"

I stare. How come I never noticed that before? I lift up the corner. Sure enough, a master carpenter has built a rectangular framed recess so that the top of the rug is exactly level with the floor around it. No wonder the faded spot is so precise. The carpet never moves, so the beam of sunlight always strikes it at exactly the same point.

I squat down beside Keenan. "There has to be some-thing under it."

Together, we lift the carpet out of the recess and gaze down at the wood underneath it.

It looks like a trapdoor. But it isn't.

We try to pry it open. It won't budge. We knock to see if it's hollow. No dice. It turns out to be exactly what it appears to be: a section of hardwood half an inch lower than the rest of the floor.

"Sorry, Keenan," I mumble. "I really thought we'd found something."

Defeated, he picks up the rug to replace it. But he pauses and holds it up for closer examination. "I *know* this," he murmurs, half under his breath. "This is familiar."

"Just a carpet," I tell him, still smarting with disap-pointment.

"No—" He gets up and crosses the living room, holding the carpet in front of him. Carefully he places the rectangular piece corner to corner against the antique map on the wall. It's a perfect fit.

I don't get it. "So they're the same size. So what?"

Keenan tosses the carpet aside. "We both looked for an X marks the spot and came up empty," he explains breathlessly. "But what if our X isn't drawn by a pencil or a pen."

When I realize what he's saying, my heart jumps into my throat. "I don't know if we can take the map out of the frame. It's over a hundred years old. If it crumbles, my folks will kill me."

He looks super tense. "It's your call, ZeeBee. But if we don't try it, we'll never know."

That does it for me. We *have* to know. "For Barney," I say.

Keeping an ear out for my parents' footsteps on the basement stairs, we unhook the frame from the wall and set it facedown on the floor. It's a delicate operation—and not just because the antique map is probably fragile. The last thing we need is for a huge chunk of cracked glass to break loose and shatter on the floor.

Keenan removes the backing to reveal the parchment, ancient and yellowed. I touch it with my forefinger. It doesn't disintegrate. That's a good sign. As gently as I can, I pick at the top right corner, separating the map from the glass. The paper feels brittle, but it holds together, and comes away in one piece.

I look at Keenan. He avoids my eyes, his gaze focused on the task at hand. There's a line of sweat across his forehead and I bet I've got a matching one.

Slowly—agonizingly slowly—I draw the parchment out of the frame and hold it up. My arms are almost at full extension, and I have to will my hands not to tremble. Keenan takes over one side, and together we're able to turn the map around so we're facing the printed side.

In lockstep, we carry the parchment over to the recess in the living room floor and lower it gently inside. The fit is perfect. There's no question that the space was custom made exactly for this map—either that, or it's the greatest coincidence in the history of home building.

We're both panting with exertion, like we've just moved a hundred-pound slab of granite, not a feather-light square of paper.

"Now what?" he asks.

"We wait." I consult the clock on the wall. A little after four. "I'd still be on the ferry right now. I don't think we've missed it."

So we sit there, cross-legged, on the hardwood floor, barely daring to breathe. I've got one eye on the stained-glass window, the other on the basement stairs. How I would explain this to my parents I have no idea. *It's called map-staring, Mum and Dad. It's the latest craze. All the kids are doing it these days.* Luckily, there's still plenty of mess in the basement to keep the folks occupied down there. And we don't have to explain ourselves to Barney Two, who's hunkered down beside us, watching the map as if he understands what's going on. (Believe me, he understands less than nothing.)

Fifteen minutes go by. Then half an hour. "Could I be remembering wrong?" I fret.

"Shhh!" Keenan warns. Like I'm jinxing us.

Barney Two spots it a split second before we do and barks one short yap.

The late-afternoon sun arcs into exactly the right position and its rays find the stained-glass window of our house. The clear center of the flower concentrates the light into a narrow beam like a laser. Outlined by swirling dust particles, it crosses the living room and bears down on the map framed on the floor.

Keenan is triumphant. "There it is, ZeeBee!"

Just as it faded a dot into that carpet square, the focused beam projects a tiny point onto the old parchment.

Trembling with anticipation, I lean closer to it. The light is focused on a spot south of Centrelight in the St. Clair River. "Wait—why would Tommy-Gun Ferguson hide his gold in the middle of the river?"

"Huh?" Quickly, Keenan picks up the map and reverses it in the rectangular space. Now the beam falls squarely on the north end of the island, right along the Canada–U.S. border, just beyond the lighthouse.

His voice is hushed with wonder. "X marks the spot!"

"I can't believe it," I whisper. Even though this is what we've been looking for, now that it's in front of us, it doesn't seem real.

Keenan produces his phone and snaps pictures of the map with its secret dot. I do the same as a backup in case his don't come out.

I'm so lost in wonder that I almost don't notice the footsteps on the basement stairs.

"My folks!" I hiss.

Remember the gentleness we used to get the map from its frame to the spot on the floor? Well, we trade all that for speed when we reverse the process. We're still hanging it up when Mum and Dad appear at the top of the landing, laden with stuffed garbage bags.

"We were trying to get the broken glass out," I explain. "But we were afraid to damage the map."

It sounds like the lamest thing in the world, but they buy it. Either that, or there's so much on their minds that they don't notice.

Keenan and I go up to the cupola to discuss our next move. The exhilaration of our momentous discovery is starting to falter, to be replaced by the practical question: What now? Even though we started out this morning with the goal of learning the secret location of Tommy-Gun's gold, neither of us actually expected to pull it off. So whatever plan we might have started out with, we're way past that now.

Sitting on the hard floor, since there's no more beanbag chair, we scroll through the photographs on our phones. It's all there: the map; the dot. We didn't imagine any of it.

"Okay, we found it," I say. "But how do we know the burglar didn't find it too?"

"Impossible," he decides. "The burglar was there at night, when there was no sun. Besides, why trash a whole house if you've already got what you're looking for?"

"So—" My words are quiet but they seem to echo as I wrap my brain around their meaning. "—millions of dollars' worth of gold are stashed somewhere out past the lighthouse and *we're* the only people who know where?"

"Unless somebody else got there first," he agrees. "It's been a long time since Tommy-Gun put it there."

He takes a deep breath. "There's only one way to find out."

As soon as he says it, I know what has to be done. I knew it the moment that beam of light kissed the parchment of the map.

I'll never be able to bring my Barney back. But if his killer was after this gold, there is one way to make that person suffer.

By beating him to it.

26

Keenan

've picked up a few choice skills in the course of my travels around the world. I can decode the colored spaghetti of a big city subway map in no time, navigate any airport like a pro, and can ask directions to a train station or a bathroom in seven different languages. I learned jai alai in Peru, Celtic dance in Ireland, and tae kwon do in Korea—although I still haven't gotten back to my old high-kicking level. I learned how to crack open a coconut using nothing but my bare hands, and maybe a rock if there's one handy.

The one skill I never mastered—something I never dreamed I'd need—is the ability to ride a bike while balancing a shovel on my lap. Dad's only shovel is the old-fashioned kind, with a heavy wooden handle and a scoop that's solid steel. Every time I pedal, the thing threatens to overbalance and put me in the ditch. The worst part is it's after midnight, and there's very little moon. So I won't even see the ditch until it eats me.

Somehow, I manage to make it to ZeeBee's house without killing myself or losing the shovel. I wait, shivering inside my jacket. The night isn't that cold, but riding a bike automatically deducts thirty degrees from the temperature. What feels like a light breeze is suddenly an arctic gale blowing in from the North Pole.

Stopped in the cover of the bushes just beyond the Tices' driveway, I check the time on my phone: 12:18. ZeeBee's late. From the moment we put this plan together, I agonized over every tiny detail that could go wrong. Except one: It never crossed my mind that ZeeBee might not show up. But now, faced with the reality, it makes perfect sense. Their house was just burglarized, their possessions trashed. It stands to reason that they're not relaxed and ready to get a good night's sleep. For all I know, Officer Tice is going to pull an all-nighter in the living room, watching for intruders. How will ZeeBee sneak out then?

I'm so lost in worst-case scenarios that when a hand closes on my wrist, I have to smother a terrified scream.

"I thought they'd never go to sleep," ZeeBee tells me in a low voice.

I adjust my shovel and try to pretend I wasn't about to swing it at her. "Way to sneak up on a guy!" I complain.

"Nice shovel," she approves. "Old-school, like mine. I think it might have been Tommy-Gun's. That would be cool—digging up his gold with the very same shovel he buried it with."

"If we find anything at all," I remind her grimly.

As we mount our bikes, I hear a rustling in the leaves behind us. "What was that?" I wheeze, terrified.

Barney Two bursts out of the bushes and runs up to ZeeBee.

"Oh no, you don't," she tells him. "This mission is going to be hard enough without having to worry about you."

Either the spaniel doesn't get the message or he

refuses to accept it. He positions himself by her front tire, raring to go.

ZeeBee dismounts and grabs him by the collar. "No way, buster. You're going back in the house."

"I don't know, ZeeBee," I say. "Maybe it's a good idea to have a watchdog with us."

"Yeah, well, if you find one, let me know." She starts to lead him up the path.

"Cut it out," I snap. "I'm sick of you putting this little guy down. He can't help the fact that he isn't Barney One. All he wants is to be with you. And if we don't let him, he might kick up a fuss and wake your folks."

That does it for ZeeBee. "Fine, he'll be our 'watchdog.'" She makes air quotes with her fingers.

She gets back on her bike and rides off to the north, Barney Two running at her side. Now not only is she annoyed with the dog; she's annoyed with me. Not exactly the smooth start I was hoping for.

I can't speak for ZeeBee's technique opening coconuts, but she's a lot better than I am at riding a bike while carrying a shovel. I have to pedal like crazy to keep up. It's more than pride that prevents me from falling behind. It's so dark that if I lose her, I might never find her again. I keep my eyes locked on the faint red glimmer of the reflector on the back of her bike seat.

Centerlight was pretty deserted during my last late-night lighthouse ride, after Ronnie's get-together. This is later still, and the island is absolutely dead. We don't see a single pedestrian or car, even when we cut through the north side of downtown. Shanghai is open twenty-four hours, and even the smaller schools Mom and Klaus have taught at are in pretty big cities. The darkness only exaggerates my sense of being alone in the universe. It's an eerie feeling, creepy almost. I keep reminding myself that it's better this way. We're going after a fortune in gold. That much money attracts the attention of ruthless people—the kind of people who don't think twice about breaking into a house or poisoning a dog.

Of course, there's no guarantee we're actually going to find anything. That beam of light projecting its point onto the map—it seemed so definite, so obvious eight hours ago. But when you're riding through the middle of nowhere in the pitch black, a cold wind blasting you out of your seat while a ten-ton shovel batters your knees, it feels like the height of crazy. Gangster treasure? What are we thinking? And as easy as it would be to blame ZeeBee, tonight is at least 60 percent my idea.

We've been pedaling for about twenty minutes when the pavement gives way to dirt road. This must be the path that leads out to the lighthouse. It's a good thing ZeeBee found it, because I lost my bearings as soon as we left downtown. The rough surface slows ZeeBee down and I'm finally able to pull even with her and Barney Two.

"You okay?" I call.

"Of course I am."

She sounds determined, but there's nervousness in her voice as well. Good. I'm not the only one.

Soon the flash of the lighthouse plays across the treetops and the old building looms ahead of us. A few minutes later, we're in the clearing, resting our bikes against the stone base. Barney Two is panting, but he looks up questioningly, game for any adventure.

"What are you so gung ho about, birdbrain?" Zee-Bee mutters at him.

He wags his tail happily.

I take out my phone and call up the map photo. The sunbeam hit the parchment almost exactly an inch and three-quarters from the lighthouse. There's no scale printed on the map. But based on the dimensions of the island, we calculated that our destination should be about 325 feet from here in a path somewhere between east-southeast and due east.

I switch my phone to compass mode and we set off in that direction, shovels over our shoulders. Barney Two bounces enthusiastically at our feet.

"How do we know how far to go?" ZeeBee asks.

"We'll count," I reply. "A short step where my heel comes down about two inches ahead of my toe is almost exactly a foot."

She frowns. "Not very exact."

I shrug. "Neither is your stained-glass window. But if we can get ourselves between ten and fifteen feet of the right place, we should be good. We've got all night to dig."

By step number thirty, we're into the woods. Almost immediately, maintaining our direction becomes a problem, because trees and underbrush are everywhere, mostly in our way. The compass keeps us on track, and between the two of us, we maintain the count.

"Fifty-two . . . fifty-three . . ."

Barney Two yaps along with us, as if he's counting.

Another problem: The farther we get from the lighthouse, the more we're affected by its powerful beacon. Each flash turns night into day, momentarily blinding us. Our progress slows to a crawl.

"Sixty-five . . . sixty-six . . ."

A worried whimper comes from Barney Two, one that turns into a little growl.

"What are you complaining about?" ZeeBee grumbles at him. "Nobody gave *you* a shovel to carry."

Then it happens. The next explosion of light outlines two figures directly in our path.

ZeeBee clamps on to my arm in a death grip and I take a step back.

Another flash, and the figures are even closer, two silhouettes, arms raised menacingly, clawlike fingers reaching for us. Barney Two buries his face in Zee-Bee's shoes.

Terror rips through me. These must be the burglars who trashed the Tice home! They've been watching the place ever since, and have followed us here in the hope that we'll lead them to the gold!

"Who are you?" ZeeBee shouts defiantly as the figures disappear into blackness once again. "What do you want?"

The reply is a burst of evil cackling laughter. I'm about to grab ZeeBee and run for our lives, but something stops me. The laughter—it sounds kind of *familiar.*

The beacon lights up again, and there they are, standing directly in front of us—Ronnie and Joey, falling all over each other with hilarity.

"Classic!" Ronnie whoops. "Absolutely classic! You should have seen the looks on your faces!"

"I hope you brought a change of underwear!" Joey adds, barely able to speak.

ZeeBee starts to swing at him with her shovel, but I stop her just in time.

"You *idiots*!" I rage at the newcomers. "What are you doing out here in the middle of the night?"

"What are *we* doing here?" Joey retorts. "What are *you* doing here?"

"None of your business!" ZeeBee hisses.

"In case you've forgotten, sweetie," Ronnie drawls at me, "we come out here all the time. We like to cut loose every now and then, unlike a certain boring person who *used* to be cool."

Joey reaches into a paper bag and comes up with a thick tangle of red firecrackers all strung together. "I was going to set these off in church, but Father Pat said find someplace else. That's why we're here. What's your excuse—and why the shovels?"

Now that my heart is back to its normal rhythm, I can think a little more clearly. Unlucky as it is to run into Ronnie and Joey, things could be a lot worse. Nobody followed us; we're not in any danger; and we're still on the trail of Tommy-Gun's gold. I even remember what step we're at: sixty-six—or maybe sixty-five; I might have jumped back a little when they startled me. It does us no good to fight with these two doofuses. We have to make peace, let them have their fun, and get back to our search.

I manufacture a smile. "All right, nice one, you guys. You really got us. So go back to the lighthouse and set off your firecrackers. I promise we won't rat you out."

Ronnie doesn't take the bait. "I know what you're doing. If Zarabeth's here, it has to have something to do with gangsters."

Joey snaps his fingers. "You're digging up gangster bones. That's what the shovels are for. And the dog's here to sniff them out for you."

"You're delusional," ZeeBee accuses. "This dog couldn't sniff out a hamburger if you put it in his dish."

Ronnie ignores her. "Which gangster, huh? Who did you find? Al Capone?"

"Al Capone died in prison," I point out. "In California."

"No way are you guys going to raid a gangster grave without us," Joey says positively. "That's way better than firecrackers. Count us in."

I catch a surreptitious headshake from ZeeBee. Her message is clear. Under no circumstances do we make these two clowns our partners. I agree with her. This gold—if we find it—is a major part of island history, and there's no way Ronnie and Joey would be mature enough to take it seriously. It's also connected to the break-in at ZeeBee's house, and, before that, Barney's poisoning. We can't forget that Ronnie's dad used to be one of our prime suspects. There's no evidence to tie him to the gold. But that doesn't change the fact that he had a grudge against Barney and that he was missing from the community hall meeting for a suspicious amount of time.

On the other hand, what are we supposed to do? Go home and come back another night? I suppose if the gold has been there more than eighty years, a few more days won't matter. But the thought of doing *this* again—the midnight bike ride with the shovels in our laps! Surely there's some way to ditch these guys and finish this now. The question is how?

It comes to me. Ronnie and Joey are relentless when it comes to having a good time, but they have the attention span of gnats.

"Awesome," I say, "it'll be good to have your help." I stifle a cry of pain when ZeeBee whacks me in the ankle with her shovel. "So we're not sure how many dead gangsters are buried here, but this is how we figure out where to dig . . ."

I launch into a long explanation that's based on the math we used to calculate the scale of ZeeBee's map, only I make it way more complicated, adding details about the curvature of the earth, the current of the St. Clair River, and the effect of the tides on Lake Huron.

ZeeBee clues in and starts talking about finding the right direction between east-southeast and due east, and what degrees and minutes mean.

Joey's eyes glaze over first. "I thought we were digging for bones, man. This sounds too much like school."

"It's *exactly* like school," I agree enthusiastically. "It's math and geography and physics—"

"Don't forget geology," ZeeBee adds. "We might have to dig our way through a lot of rock."

Ronnie rolls his eyes. "Come on, Joey. Who cares about a bunch of old bones? Let's go make some noise."

Without another word, the two take off in the direction of the lighthouse to set off their firecrackers.

We can still hear them talking about it as they disappear into the trees.

"Give me the matches."

"I thought *you* had the matches . . ."

Barney Two barks softly in their general direction, as if to say . . . *And don't come back!*

"My hero," ZeeBee says sarcastically. "This stinks! I thought we'd be all alone out here."

"Let's just keep going," I advise, resuming our march to 325. "By the time we get to the right spot and start digging, they'll never find us again."

But as we forge on, counting past 100, 150, 200, I actually begin to miss Ronnie and Joey. Without their goofy presence, the silence and darkness and isolation feel that much deeper. Even worse, with every step, I'm bracing myself for the earsplitting detonation of firecrackers. The longer it doesn't happen, the more I'm dreading it.

ZeeBee reads my mind. "You think those two idiots really did forget the matches?"

"I wouldn't put it past them," I reply. "They're probably rubbing two sticks together right now."

I step over a low shrub and count 300. "Twenty-five feet to go."

The searchlight passes over us again. As it does, we can look ahead twenty-five feet and more. I don't know what I'm expecting to see—maybe a sign: HERE IT IS—TOMMY-GUN'S GOLD, with an arrow pointing straight down. That would be very helpful.

Instead, the final paces bring us to a place that looks exactly like the rest of the woods—trees, underbrush, vines, rocks, and ground. Lots of ground. Barney Two licks at a weed, thinks it over, and turns his nose up at it.

I bury my shovel in the forest floor experimentally. It's a lot harder than I expected. "Now what?"

She starts turning the earth. "We dig."

I get to work with Dad's heavy shovel. Within thirty seconds, the windy cold of the bike ride is a distant memory, and I'm sweating like a hog. Seeing us, the spaniel finds some nice soft dirt and begins scrabbling at it with his front paws.

"Oh, that'll help," ZeeBee comments under her breath.

That brings up a good point. "How deep should we go?" I ask.

ZeeBee kicks her spade farther into the ground. "I don't know. But I'm guessing Tommy-Gun buried this by himself. It was his life savings. No way would he trust anybody else to know where it was. I'll bet it's no more than three or four feet down."

That's supposed to make me feel good. I've penetrated about eight inches and I'm ready to pass out. The problem is we don't know how far away we are from the actual gold. So that three or four feet could end up extending to a gigantic circle fifty feet wide.

To say that we dig is the understatement of the century. It's a major operation. Making things even more difficult, our shovels keep running into a spaghetti of thick roots, some from towering old trees as far as fifteen or twenty feet away. I remember something I learned in elementary school science class in Lesotho or maybe Korea: During a drought, the smaller roots will reach for the surface, where there's more moisture. Well, there must have been a lot of dry spells between now and when Tommy-Gun buried his gold, because these roots are reaching for the sky.

ZeeBee hacks at a root with the sharp edge of her spade. "This stuff is like titanium!"

"And if the gold is underneath it," I add, "we're never going to break through. Not without a jackhammer."

She doesn't answer and I don't blame her. It isn't easy to talk and shovel at the same time. You have to make an executive decision about what you choose to spend your breath on.

We dig as far as the roots will allow us, and when we can go no deeper, we widen the hole until the area is about the size of a backyard swimming pool. We have to work around trees and pull out several small shrubs. Barney Two is still "helping," although half the time, he's filling up what we've already emptied.

"Hey, cut it out," ZeeBee complains, using the point of her shovel to flick some soft earth at him.

The spaniel jumps away, and when he lands in the hole, there's a soft clicking sound—the dog's nails against a hard surface. It isn't very loud, but we both notice it because it's so different from what we've been hearing since the dig began.

"A big rock?" she muses.

We jump in after the dog to investigate. There's the clicking again as Barney Two paws at something sticking out of the ground.

Something metal.

27

Keenan

ZeeBee and I drop to our knees over the hole. That sound wasn't made by Barney Two's nails against a root or stone that would appear naturally on Centerlight. There's metal down there!

With our bare hands, we clear the dirt away to reveal a section of worn and tarnished brass, exactly the shape of one of the protective corners on a piece of old-fashioned luggage.

"A steamer trunk!" I exclaim. I've seen a million of them on my travels with Mom and Klaus.

I would have bet money that ZeeBee and I had no strength left. But we fall on the buried trunk with shovels flying. Barney Two runs for cover to protect himself from the blizzard of earth that's storming all around us. Pretty soon we've got the lid uncovered. I try to pull whatever it is out by its leather handle. It won't budge, not even an eighth of an inch.

So we go back to digging, and there's no question that we've found some kind of chest or trunk that's been buried a long time. The wood construction has deteriorated over the years, but the brass cladding still holds everything together. A large rusted padlock fastens the metal clasp.

ZeeBee is practically beside herself. "Is there a name on it? An address—*my* address? Initials—T.F.? Anything?"

I shake my head. "I don't think so. But that doesn't mean it was never there. It could have faded over time."

"It must be the gold," she persists. "What else could it be?"

"We have to open it," I decide, pulling at the padlock to see if the rust has loosened it. No luck. Undaunted,

I poke at the clasp with the corner of Dad's shovel.

ZeeBee is bubbling over with impatience. "Come on, Keenan, you've got to put some muscle into it!"

She cocks back her spade like a baseball bat and unloads a home-run swing. I barely get out of the way before it would have taken my head off. The steel scoop misses the padlock entirely and buries itself in the wood of the lid.

"It's rotted right through!" I exclaim in amazement.

ZeeBee pulls her spade free and starts hacking at the trunk. I join in with my shovel. Barney Two cowers in fear behind a tree as we pound away at the old chest. When my blade finally breaks through the top, it strikes something so hard that the impact vibrates all the way up my arm to my shoulders. The *clang* echoes through the woods.

I twist my shovel and tear a large piece of shredded wood from the lid.

ZeeBee gasps, and I turn back to the chest to check out what she's looking at.

At first, it's too dark to see anything. Then, the searchlight passes overhead and the contents of the chest gleam up at me with a yellow brightness that could only be one thing.

Gold. Tommy-Gun Ferguson's secret stash—bricks

of it, packed into the buried chest.

Mouth hanging open in wonder, ZeeBee reaches in and draws out a single bar. It's so heavy that she loses her grip, and it drops to the ground. Barney Two rushes over to investigate the shiny object. Skittering through the loose earth, he runs into the gold nose-first and bounces back, stunned.

I pick up the brick with both hands. It must weigh twenty-five pounds, probably more. No wonder I couldn't lift the trunk. It isn't stuck; it's *heavy*. There have to be dozens of bars in there! I don't know how much it was worth during Prohibition, but today it would buy you a medium-sized city!

"I've never seen so much gold in my life!" ZeeBee's voice is just a whisper. "How did Tommy-Gun even carry it here?"

I shrug. "It was over eighty years ago. This whole forest probably barely existed back then. I'll bet he drove it in the trunk of his car. Chances are, he buried it deeper, but over the decades, the trees grew, and the roots pushed it up toward the surface. We were lucky to find it."

Barney Two begins to bark excitedly. It seems almost like a chorus of agreement, until a voice from some-where behind us comes out of the darkness:

"Maybe not so lucky as you think."

We wheel in the direction of the speaker, but at that moment, a powerful flashlight beam blinds us both.

"Ronnie?" I ask. "Joey? That you guys?" Although part of me already knows that the voice is too deep to belong to one of them.

"Step away from the gold!" orders a second voice, this one definitely familiar.

I rack my brain to conjure up a face to go with it. The suspect list—I've met them all, talked with them. It can't be Ms. Batista or one of the Quayle sisters. The newcomers are both male. I sift through my memory, trying to bring up tone, timbre, enunciation. Mr. Chaiken? Mr. Piccoli? What about Mr. Lindahl? I think back to how he sounded when he snatched Ronnie off the street on water balloon day.

Then the flashlight lowers and a man steps into our line of vision. It's Mr. Tolenski.

I'm stunned. Sure, Mr. Tolenski was one of the original suspects, but we took him off the list. At the same time, I wonder how I could have missed this. Peter Tolenski's last book was about searching for lost treasure. I feel the weight of the heavy gold bar in my hands. If this doesn't count as treasure, nothing does.

"But you never left the meeting at the community hall!" ZeeBee exclaims. "You couldn't have poisoned Barney!"

"Ah, the dog." The writer seems genuinely regretful. "I was not the one who performed that unpleasant task."

"*I* was." The second man steps out of the shadows. Broad shoulders, big muscles, much younger.

"Bryce!" My fitness trainer. My *friend*!

Bryce shoots me a crooked smile. "Small world, huh, Keenan?"

I'm too shocked to reply.

"Nothing personal," he assures me. "Peter and I had our eyes on this gold long before your old man ever sent you to me. We just had to figure out how to get rid of the mutt."

"He had a *name*," ZeeBee says, her voice quavering yet strong. "He was Barney, and he wouldn't hurt a *fly*."

"Oh really?" Bryce holds out his beefy arm, displaying the jagged scar that cuts through his tattoo. "Does this count?"

"You told me it was an MMA injury!" I should have

known! That's an angry scar—a *fresh* scar! Not one from a long time ago.

He walks up to me and snatches the gold out of my hands. "You can't believe everything you hear. I said you were good at tae kwon do too. I say a lot of things—to get what I want."

"Now who's making excuses?" I demand bitterly.

He snorts a short, humorless laugh. "You always were a smart kid. Too smart for your own good."

Even though we've been training together for over a month, it's the first time I truly understand how big he is, and how powerful. He's nearly a foot taller than me and must outweigh me by a hundred pounds. He handles the heavy metal brick like it's a stick of gum.

"It was unfortunate that the dog had to go," Mr. Tolenski interrupts. "But we needed to get into your house, and the big brute made that impossible."

"Unfortunate?" Bryce sneers. "Half this island would give me a parade if they knew I was the one who took down that hellhound!"

ZeeBee's face flames red. "He wasn't a hellhound—"

"ZeeBee," I whisper desperately, "*no!*"

But she isn't hearing me anymore. She's just too upset. She runs at Bryce, pummeling him with both fists, and becomes even more enraged when all he does is laugh. Finally, tiring of her attack, the bodybuilder gives her a mighty shove that sends her sprawling.

The bark torn from Barney Two is much louder than any sound he's ever made before. I also never knew he could fly. In defense of his beloved ZeeBee, the little spaniel closes the distance to Bryce in a fraction of a second and leaps on the bewildered giant, burying his teeth in the already scarred forearm.

Bryce howls in agony, trying to shake the little dog off. Barney Two, snarling and growling, is clamped on like a crocodile and refuses to let go. The trainer swipes at him with his free hand, but he's still holding on to the heavy brick, so his movements are hampered.

At last, Mr. Tolenski joins the fray. He grabs Barney Two by the hindquarters and twists him off Bryce's arm. Now free of the little dog's bite, Bryce stalks forward. The fury of his expression is terrifying to watch. He raises the gold bar, and his intention is all too clear. He's going to bring it down on the head of the dog that dared to attack him.

It brings a scream from ZeeBee. "Stop!"

What happens next is the last thing anybody could

possibly have expected. A rapid-fire series of crackling explosions fills the air, freezing us into a shocked diorama. The lighthouse beam sweeps overhead, providing a momentary view of a cascade of firecrackers bursting all around us. Over the loud pops, I can hear Ronnie and Joey, yelling instructions to each other, but I can't take my eyes off the gold brick that's about to crush the skull of that brave little dog.

I don't think; I just react. Like a coiling spring, I twirl around into the familiar tae kwon do stance, and my leg launches out into the kick I haven't been able to execute since I got sick. My whole body tenses as I strain to reach the height that has eluded me so far.

Whack!

The sole of my sneaker smacks into the heavy piece of gold, ramming it into the side of Bryce's head. I'm aware of an eruption of pain in my foot, but I barely even notice. My only thought is on saving Barney Two.

Bryce's eyes roll back and he crumples, unconscious, to the dirt. That's the last thing I see before I hit the ground myself. I land at the feet of Mr. Tolenski, who is standing there like a statue, still holding Barney Two.

ZeeBee struggles off the ground. "Get your filthy hands off my dog!" she snarls at Mr. Tolenski, launching herself like a linebacker. She hits him just below the knees, toppling him full length in the dirt. Barney Two leaps free and runs over to ZeeBee, who's still clamped on to the writer's ankles.

Mr. Tolenski tries to scramble up, but at that moment, Ronnie and Joey burst out of the trees and jump on top of him.

"Don't even think about it, mister!" Ronnie barks. "The cops are almost here."

The writer pushes them off. "Exactly how stupid do you think I am?"

The beam of a high-powered flashlight cuts through the trees. "All right, you two. You've had your fun—"

The late arrival stops dead in his tracks and takes in the scene: Bryce's mammoth form, out cold; me, sitting up, but unable to rise. Mr. Tolenski, with Ronnie and Joey clamped on to him and ZeeBee at his feet.

Officer Darryl Tice of the Canadian Border Service stares at his daughter. "ZeeBee, what are you doing here? I thought you were in bed!"

Joey snickers. "She's in trouble."

ZeeBee stands, picking up Barney Two in her arms.

"Dad, these two guys"—indicating Bryce and Mr. Tolenski—"they're the ones who murdered Barney. Oh yeah, and we also found Tommy-Gun Ferguson's gold."

Her father flushes with impatience. "Not now, Zee—"

At that moment, his flashlight beam passes over the broken lid of the steamer trunk, and the contents gleam back at him.

To illustrate the point, I pick up the bar I kicked into Bryce's face. "It's all true. These are also the guys who broke into your house."

"Lies!" Mr. Tolenski stands up and brushes himself off. "I'm a treasure hunter. There's no crime in that. I was after the gold when I was attacked by these children."

ZeeBee's dad strolls over to him. "Yeah, they can be kind of a handful—especially my daughter." There are two sharp clicks and the next thing we know, Mr. Tolenski is in handcuffs.

It gets kind of crazy after that. Officer Tice radios for backup. He also calls an ambulance for Bryce and—it turns out—me. My foot hurts so bad that I can't even stand. When I take my sneaker off, I'm purple and swollen from toes to ankle.

The police arrive—more Canadian border officers, and the island cops from Centerlight, Michigan, P.D. Despite the fact that a whole lot of crimes have been committed, and Mr. Tolenski and Bryce are under arrest, all anyone seems to care about is the gold.

Parents are contacted, Ronnie's, Joey's, and my father. Dad will have to meet me at the hospital, in the X-ray department of the emergency room.

"Hope your foot's okay," Ronnie tells me before he and Joey start back to the lighthouse, where Mr. Lindahl is coming to pick them up.

"Thanks," I reply. "Do you think you guys are in trouble because of the firecrackers?"

"Nah," Joey scoffs. "Adults are so obsessed with worst-case scenarios. Just because you've got fire in a forest doesn't mean there's going to be a forest fire."

They also stop and ask ZeeBee if she's okay, which I wasn't expecting. I don't think she was either.

ZeeBee hasn't let go of Barney Two for one second since the action started. While officials from two countries are wrangling over how to get an ambulance into the woods and more than half a ton of gold out, she sits with her back against a tree, cradling the spaniel in her arms.

"You know, the dog's got legs," I tell her, amused.

"He chased your bike all the way out here. He can walk."

"Heroes don't have to walk," she replies smugly. "Isn't that right, Barney?" She buries her face in his rich blond fur and plants a long kiss on his snout. The spaniel wriggles with pure happiness.

I'm taken aback. "Wow, that's the first time you've ever called him Barney."

She looks defensive. "Why wouldn't I? That's his name, isn't it?"

28

Zarabeth

Keenan has two fractured metatarsals.

I don't understand why he can't just call it a broken foot. It's like every time he has a medical problem, there has to be a fancy, complicated name for it. First tuberculosis and now this.

What's the big deal? His foot hurts. It'll get better. Right now they've got him in a boot, and he has to use crutches to get around. He didn't even spend the night in the hospital. Not like that Bryce guy. It might be a week before he can remember what happened to him. I guess the moral of the story is if you have to choose a part of the body to slam into a solid gold brick, your foot is better than your head.

But even if Bryce was totally okay, he wouldn't be going anywhere anytime soon. He and Mr. Tolenski are both under arrest for attempted assault and child endangerment, us being the endangered children. Dad says there are going to be other charges too, like breaking into our house and murdering old Barney. That's probably just going to be called animal cruelty, depending on whether the crime took place in Canada or the United States. (That's always an issue on Centrelight.) The good news is that police on both sides of the border are almost as mad at those two crooks as I am. Too bad Eliot Ness died a long time ago, because nobody arrested more criminals around here than he did. But I'm pretty sure that Dad and the Michigan cops will do a good job.

I just wish they could get their minds off the dumb *gold*.

The thing about the gold is there's a lot of it—1,320 pounds, worth about twenty-six million American dollars, and even more in Canadian. And no one can be sure which country owns it yet, since it was buried so close to the border. Next week they're bringing in map surveyors to figure out which side it was on. They could have just asked me. I'm positive they're going to find out that the gold was buried exactly on the border—half in one country, half in the other. It's Tommy-Gun Ferguson's style. I should know. I've lived in his house since the day I was born.

On the other hand, I'm done with treating gangsters like Tommy-Gun and Al Capone and Lucky Luciano and all those others as if they were larger-than-life heroes. Oh sure, their names bring in a lot of tourists and make Centrelight seem important and fun. But now that I've seen real criminals up close and personal, I've stopped thinking those guys were ever cool. When I remember what Bryce and Tolenski did to poor old Barney, it makes my blood boil.

If I didn't have my awesome new dog (Barney), I don't know what I'd do.

Because Keenan is on crutches, I have to dig the grave myself.

As I proved that night out by the lighthouse, I'm a pretty good digger. And anyway, this is kind of easy. You don't need a very deep hole to bury field mice, garter snakes, squirrels, chipmunks, and birds.

The whole idea started when Keenan got the piece of poisoned meat out of his sock drawer and gave it to my dad to be used as evidence of the animal cruelty charges. We decided to have a "funeral" for all the little animals that died from nibbling at what was left of the steak that was used to kill old Barney.

The grave is at the very far corner of our yard, right next to where the first Barney is buried. I don't come here very much. It brings back such sad memories. Dad had to rent a backhoe to dig a hole big enough. "It's like burying an elephant," I overheard him saying to Mum, which was pretty hurtful at the time.

It took Dad and four guys from work to carry the burlap sack with poor old Barney in it (he weighed almost two hundred pounds). Dad joked that if there was ever a good day to smuggle something into Canada, this was it, because the whole border service was in our yard. I didn't think that was funny either.

Dad replanted the grass, and it's growing pretty well over the mound. The only thing that needs to be changed is the marker I put up, handwritten on a piece of two-by-four: I WILL NEVER LOVE ANOTHER DOG.

Okay, that's wrong. I didn't know it then, but I know it now.

I look over at my new dog. Barney stands at attention next to Keenan on his crutches. Even though he can't possibly understand what's really going on, the cocker spaniel can tell that this is a solemn moment. He's not only a hero; he's a canine genius.

Keenan's not so bad himself. If he hadn't sacrificed his foot by kicking that gold bar into Bryce's head, I might have lost two Barneys instead of just one.

I'll never forget the first time I spotted Keenan on that lawn chair in his father's backyard. I couldn't have known back then how important our friendship was going to be. But even on that day, I sensed he was a good guy.

Keenan hands me the flat carton that holds the remains of all those little animals, and I set it down into the hole. We don't say any words, but we bury them with respect. (Even the snakes.)

"I'm glad we did that," Keenan tells me when it's over and we're walking back to the house. Actually, *I'm* walking. He's hobbling. The guy may have a good tae kwon do kick, but he stinks on crutches.

Then he says, "Ronnie's having some people over on Saturday."

"Another party?"

"Call it a get-together. He doesn't like the P-word."

I scowl. "And I should care about this because . . . ?"

"Well, for one thing, because he wants you to come."

I'm sarcastic. "Yeah, sure."

"It's true," he insists. "He said it outright: *Bring Zarabeth.*"

"I don't trust him," I snap. "Why should I go?"

"Well, we kind of owe him, when you think about it. He and Joey saved our necks that night with their firecrackers."

"I don't care," I retort. "He only wants me there to make fun of me."

He spreads his arms wide. "Don't you get it? What were the reasons those kids thought you were weird? You said your dog was murdered. News flash—that turned out to be one hundred percent true! You talked about gangster gold. Guess what—we just pulled twenty-six million dollars' worth of it out of the ground. You're the *opposite* of weird, ZeeBee. You're the only one who had a clue!"

Funny, in all the chaos of the other night, it never occurred to me that everything that happened showed that I was *right*—about old Barney, about Tommy-Gun's gold, and even the idea that someone was spying on our house. This proves that I'm not crazy—which

I knew all along. But for everybody else, it's a big change.

"So you're saying I should go to Ronnie's to rub it in those guys' faces," I conclude.

"*Or*"—the famous brow rises—"you could use this as a chance to start over with them the way they're using it as a chance to start over with you."

Keenan talks like a guidance counselor sometimes.

"They probably think I kept all the gold, so they only want to be friends with me because I'm rich. When they find out I don't get a nickel, they'll drop me like a hot potato."

"Trust me," Keenan assures me. "They don't think that, because I told them I don't get a nickel either. Give them a break, ZeeBee. They're not bad people."

"Fine, I'll go." Just because you sound like a guidance counselor doesn't mean you're wrong *all* the time. Besides, it's not like I have to meet new people. I've known most of these kids since we were babies together. We just went off track since I split from them for school, because of which side of the border I live on.

In the end, what's a border, really? A white line some guy painted way back when. Big deal.

29

Keenan

Tommy-Gun Ferguson's gold makes the news in Shanghai.

I'm blown away when Mom and Klaus call me on Skype to let me know that little Centerlight is in all the Chinese papers. But ZeeBee isn't surprised at all.

"Gangsters are *interesting*," she explains.

Those three words tell you almost everything you need to know about Zarabeth Tice. Back on day one, she hadn't been in our yard more than thirty seconds before I figured out that much about her.

The gangster gold has made ZeeBee almost a legend among the kids of Centerlight. I don't care about that, but it's great to see people finally getting her. It doesn't hurt that Barney—formerly Barney Two—is so lovable that people are starting to forget his predecessor. Plus Officer Tice's back bacon on a bun has become so famous at my school that people line up for invitations to ZeeBee's family barbecues.

It bugs me a little that I used to be the only person the cocker spaniel could turn to for affection, but now he's got fans all over the island. In the end, though, none of us can compete with his number-one fan, ZeeBee herself. Fair enough. The poor little guy more than earned it.

Of course, Mom and Klaus already knew about the gold by the time it hit the Chinese papers. Dad called them that night—daytime in Shanghai—to tell them I was in the hospital because I broke my foot kicking a gold bar. Mom had a few things to say about that, none of them quiet. But even she had to admit that a broken foot isn't as bad as tuberculosis.

It hurts like crazy, though.

Today's conversation with Mom is harder than the

broken foot one, because today is when I give her the news that I'm not going back to Shanghai. That's the plan Dad and I worked out after the long lecture about being crazy enough to sneak out and dig up gangster gold in the dead of night.

I think he's actually looking forward to having a permanent roommate. For sure he's happy that all I wound up with was a broken foot, as opposed to a broken head—or worse.

It's nothing against Mom and Klaus. I loved my life traveling from city to city with them and seeing the world. The only problem is you don't really have a home. I used to be okay with that, since I never knew what I was missing. But here on Centerlight, I've found it.

Sure, I'll still visit. Maybe I'll travel with them on school breaks. But I have Dad and ZeeBee and Barney and my friends from school. I have the ghosts of dozens of Prohibition gangsters, including Tommy-Gun Ferguson—although *his* ghost is a lot poorer than he used to be. This rock gets under your skin. I'm an islander now.

Mom is a little choked up, but she reluctantly agrees. And Klaus is already planning a trip to Centerlight next summer to learn about the gangster days of

Prohibition and to check out Tommy-Gun Ferguson's gold.

I haven't got the heart to tell him that nobody is going to see that gold anytime soon. The results of the survey just came in, confirming that the steamer trunk was buried exactly on the borderline. So the United States and Canada are suing each other in international court over who owns it. ZeeBee's dad says the case could drag on for years.

The only thing both countries agree on is a plan to take six million dollars out of the pot to pay for all the repairs needed on the lighthouse. So Mom and Klaus might not get to view the gold, which is in a bank vault somewhere under heavy guard. But they can still visit the best lighthouse on the entire St. Clair River. Centerlight is pretty unique, even for a pair of experienced world travelers.

"You'll fall in love with the place," I promise, and can't resist adding, "just like Al Capone."

Turn the page for a sneak peek at Gordon Korman's new novel, *UNPLUGGED*.

1

JETT BARANOV

Matt says I could see the majestic beauty of the American Southeast if I'd bother to glance out the window.

So I glance. "Clouds," I report. "Whoop-de-do."

I've got all the majestic beauty I need right here. I've got a private plane, cruising at 28,000 feet. I've got two flight attendants who bring me snacks and sodas every time they think I look hungry or thirsty.

I've got superfast internet, even though we're flying way above any cell network. My phone connects to a system of satellites, thanks to a tiny chip designed by Fuego, the tech company started by my father.

Right now, the screen shows the selfie I just took, slightly enhanced using Fuego's state-of-the-art editing software. I add a caption—*Jett on a jet*. If that's not meme-worthy, I don't know what is. With a swipe, I upload it to the Fuego app.

Matt rolls his eyes when the image appears on his screen. He follows all my social media, but he's not a buddy. *Warden* might be a better word—or at least *babysitter*. My father—Matt's boss—put him in charge of keeping me out of trouble. That might be the hardest job in Silicon Valley right now. Quantum computing is patty-cake compared with trying to make me do something I don't want to. That's kind of a point of pride with me.

"Jett on a jet?" he challenges. "Really? Sixty grand a year for the finest schools and that's the best you can come up with?"

"It's insightful commentary on my life," I insist. "Dad loves this plane more than he loves me. He even named me after it."

"And the extra *T* stands for *trouble*," Matt adds,

quoting my father's often-repeated comment. Yes, the famous Vladimir Baranov, billionaire founder of Fuego, cracks dumb dad jokes like all the other fathers.

The plane's official name is the *Del Fuego*. Our forty-acre compound in Silicon Valley is known as Casa del Fuego. You get the picture. I've named my toilet the Fuego Bowl. Back in December, I set off a bunch of cherry bombs in it to see if I could trigger the Fuego Detector in the hall. Verdict: success. I also found out that our whole house is outfitted with emergency sprinklers. Vlad was pretty ticked off about that. How was I supposed to know? My family's all about Fuego, not Agua.

Come to think of it, that was just about when Matt began spending a lot more time in the company of his boss's son. Matt Louganis started out as a high-flying young programmer at Fuego. Lately, though, his job seems to be keeper.

I feel a little bad about that. Matt signed on with Fuego to change the world, not to ride with me in the limo to school to make sure I actually get there. Or to be an extra chaperone at the Halloween dance to prevent a repeat of the *last* Halloween dance, when I hired a local motorcycle gang to ride their Harleys into the gym. There were a lot of tall eighth graders last year, so it took a couple of minutes for the teachers to realize that the newcomers weren't actually students.

Hey, I'm just having fun. Sometimes, you have to work at it. It's harder than it looks, you know. I have a saying: "Fertilizer, meet fan. . . ." I originally had another word for the first part, but it already got me kicked out of my private school—my third in three years, by the way. My mother flew all the way back from Ulaanbaatar to straighten things out—starting with me.

Vlad says what I really need is to find some friends. That's also harder than it looks. People expect me to be a stuck-up rich kid, so they stay away. Whatever. I've gotten pretty good at lone-wolfing it. Too good, some people think. *Bay Area Weekly* just named me Silicon Valley's Number One Spoiled Brat. Remember, we're talking about California. Think of all the other spoiled brats I had to beat out for that title. Vlad always says I should aim for the best.

Besides, I've always got Matt. He's twenty-seven, but he still counts as a friend. I mean, I think he'd still hang out with me even if his boss didn't tell him to. Yeah, right. I'm sure he can think of a million things he'd rather do.

The pilot makes an announcement to fasten our seat belts and turn off all electronics.

As usual, I ignore both messages.

Matt's exasperated. "Your name may be Baranov, but your head can split open the same as anybody else's."

So I sigh and fasten my seat belt, but I pull a blanket over my lap so Matt won't see.

When we're on the tarmac and they open the door to let us out, the blast of heat and humidity nearly knocks me back into the galley.

"What is this place—the Amazon jungle?"

Matt grins right in my face. "Welcome to Arkansas."

"No, seriously," I tell him.

He's solemn. "This is Little Rock, Arkansas. We've still got a three-hour drive ahead of us from here."

"To where—the moon?"

He reaches back and pulls me down the stairs to the tarmac. "Listen, Jett. The sprinkler thing was bad enough. When the floors warped, your poor father had to get the replacement wood imported from specials cedars in Lebanon."

"My science teacher says a cherry bomb has more than a gram of flash powder," I explain. "Sue me for being *curious*."

Matt's not done yet. "Was it curiosity that made you

5

drive that go-kart off Fisherman's Wharf? Lucky for you I was able to kill the story before it went viral on Twitter. But when you pulled that little stunt with the drone—"

Well, you can't blame me for that. I was just trying to get a few aerial shots of Emma Loudermilk's pool party. The problem was that sitting between my house and hers is San Francisco Airport. Fertilizer, meet fan.

"That wasn't my fault," I defend myself. "How was I supposed to know the air force was going to scramble fighter planes to shoot down one little drone? Or that the pieces were going to break so many windshields in that parking lot?"

"Don't act so surprised," Matt tells me firmly, steering me toward the terminal building. "This isn't the first time your antics got you a little too much attention and you had to lie low for a while."

"Yeah," I agree. "But lying low is a couple of weeks on the Riviera or maybe Bali. Not Arizona."

"Arkansas," he corrects me.

"So who's going to know if the two of us get back on the plane, fuel up, and fly someplace decent? Remember that private surf island off Australia where everybody gets their own chef?"

He cuts me off. "Forget it, Jett. Your dad's right on

top of this. The place we're going has a waiting list—he had to pull a lot of strings to get us in this summer."

"Waiting list, huh? I like the sound of that." In Silicon Valley, if you don't have to pull strings to get into something, it probably isn't worth getting into. "What is it—some sick new resort? And they put it in Arkansas to scare away the uncool people?"

He smiles. "Something like that. Come on, the Range Rover's waiting for us."

I'm encouraged. But something about his cake-eating grin makes me uneasy. Especially when I see the car, which is splashed with mud and pockmarked in a dozen places. This isn't the kind of Range Rover from the rap songs. It's the kind you ship to Africa to drive over the elephant poop.

It's ten times hotter inside the car than outside it. The air-conditioning isn't broken; it just doesn't exist.

The driver is either named Buddy or wants us to consider him *our* buddy—I'm not sure which. He assures us we don't need air-conditioning. "A certain amount of sweating is good for you," he calls over the engine's roar. "It's part of the program—keeps your skin pores open. You're cooler in the long run."

"Program?" I ask Matt suspiciously.

He just shrugs.

7

The breeze feels like it's coming from a hair dryer set on fricassee. But after an hour on the road, I don't even care that I'm sweat-drenched from head to toe.

"Where *are* we?" I hiss. "How much worse is this going to get?"

"We're on our way," he insists, "to the—uh—resort." But he doesn't look too happy either. Maybe the bumpy two-lane road is messing with his stomach. No resort I ever went to had an approach like this.

"Couldn't we have gone by helicopter? Or float plane?"

He shakes his head. "This place is really remote."

Tell me about it. We haven't seen a solitary soul in twenty miles that didn't have feathers or four legs. This resort has a waiting list? I'd hate to see the one nobody wants to go to.

Another hour goes by. The scenery doesn't change. Standing by the side of the road, a deer looks at me as we pass by. I swear there's pity in its eyes.

There are signs that talk about towns, but we never see any. By this time, I'm not just physically miserable and bored out of my mind; I'm also starving. I'd give a thousand preferred shares of Fuego stock for a bag of Doritos. The luxury of the Gulfstream feels like it happened in another lifetime—a way better one.

Finally, three hours in, we get there. I look around for the trappings of a vacation hot spot. Palm trees, towering waterslides, gleaming hotel buildings. Nothing. There's a small sign by the main entrance:

THE OASIS OF MIND & BODY WELLNESS

I turn to Matt. "Wellness?"

"This is the place," he confirms. "Your dad set the whole thing up."

How do I even describe it? A lot of words come to mind, none of them *resort*. It's decently large, surrounded by woods, with small neat cottages dotted all over the property. There are a few bigger buildings too, but none higher than a single story. It isn't a dump. Nothing is falling apart, and it's all freshly painted and well maintained. It isn't totally un-fun. There's a pool at least—the kind any crummy motel would have. No waterslides or anything cool like that. There are people on bikes and, in the distance, kayaking and pedal boating on a lake. What can I say? It's sort of okay, but it's definitely not the kind of high-end destination where you get your own chef. My father picked this place? No way!

The driver takes us to the welcome center so we can check in.

I tug on Matt's arm. "I don't get it. Why would Vlad send me clear across the country and hours into the wilderness to a place that doesn't have anything half as good as the stuff at our own house?"

"Take it easy—"

"And what's this whole 'wellness' thing? I'm not sick!"

"We're all sick," comes a rich female voice, smooth as melted caramel, from behind the counter. "In fact, the moment we're born, we immediately begin dying."

Picture the most intimidating woman you've ever seen—like a supermodel on the body of one of those female wrestlers in WWE. The figure who stands up from her chair must be six foot four, yet she carries herself with a catlike ease and grace. She has huge pale gray eyes that are closer to silver. Her hair is almost silver too—what there is of it. It's close cropped—I swear it's shorter than mine. I'm so tempted to stare at her that I have to look away.

"Uh—hi," Matt says, clearly thrown. "I'm Matt Louganis and this is Jett Baranov. Checking in."

"I envy you," the lady informs us in that almost musical tone. "No part of the journey is ever quite so eye-opening as the first step. I'm Ivory Novis. I'm in charge of meditation here."

"Meditation?" I echo.

"This is the Oasis of Mind and Body Wellness. We heal the body through diet and exercise. The mind, on the other hand, is a more complicated instrument. The valves of a trumpet can be oiled. Only meditation can tune the mind."

Huh? "I've heard of math teachers and English teachers," I tell her. "But meditation teachers? That's a new one."

"Here at the Oasis we say 'pathfinder,' not 'teacher.' I cannot plant information inside your head. I can merely show you the path to understanding."

Every time Ivory Novis opens her mouth, a lot of serious weirdness comes out. I blurt, "You know that waiting list? Is it to get in, or get out?"

Ivory laughs and then holds out her hand. Matt moves to shake it, but that's not what she has in mind.

"Your phones, gentlemen," she tells us.

A great fear clutches at my heart. "What about them?"

"You have to turn them in," Ivory explains like it's the most obvious thing in the world. "It's the one strict rule of the Oasis—no electronics. On the path to wellness, the only screen you need is the vast blank slate of your imagination."

I'm psyched. Finally we come to the part where Matt tells this Wonder Woman on steroids where she can stick her Oasis. So it's a blow when I see him hand over his beloved F-phone like it's nothing.

"You *knew* about this?" I accuse him.

He nods grimly. "And so did your father."

That's when it dawns on me. "Vlad didn't send me here to lie low. He sent me here for *revenge*! Just because he had to pay back the air force for scrambling those fighter planes."

Matt shakes his head solemnly. "Your father loves you. He sent you here because you *need* this. Silicon Valley's Number One Spoiled Brat—that looks cute in a magazine. But these stunts of yours are getting out of hand. What if a piece of that drone had gone through somebody's skull instead of just their windshield? One of these days, you're going to do something that your father can't buy you out of. He's trying to save your life, Jett. And so am I." And he plucks my phone out of my pocket and hands it to Ms. Meditation.

I fold my arms across my chest. "I'm not staying."

In answer, he reaches into my bag and pulls out my F-pad and my laptop and surrenders those too. Then he takes the smartwatch right off my wrist and tosses it across the counter.

"You're fired," I snarl.

He's patient. "Remember Liam Reardon?"

A kid in my school. His dad owns, like, half of Google. "What about him?"

"He was a zombie. He never looked away from a screen long enough to make eye contact with a real human. He was hostile. Antisocial. He'd gone through every therapist in the Bay Area and half of the ones in LA. Then his parents sent him here."

Ms. Meditation nods. "Liam. Wonderful boy. The Oasis made such a difference for him. As it will for you." The silver eyes bore into me at high intensity until I have to study my sneakers to avoid the onslaught. "The coming weeks will be the turning point of your spiritual life."

"I don't have a spiritual life," I reply stubbornly. "Some crazy lady stole it along with my phone."

If Ivory is offended by that, she doesn't let on. "Hostility is the byproduct of a mind out of balance," she says understandingly.

"At least I have a mind," I mumble under my breath.

"Don't be rude." Matt puts an arm around my shoulders in an attempt to calm me down. "Take it easy, kid. You're not in California anymore."

I shrug him off violently. "Yeah, really? What tipped you off? The swamp gas? The possum BO? The fact that we haven't seen an In-N-Out Burger for two hundred miles?"

"You must be starving," Ivory says smoothly. "I've got some good news for you there. Early dinner is being served right now. You have to try our burgers. They're world-renowned."

I struggle to get my whirling mind under control. If this was San Francisco, I'd tell everybody to stick it and Uber home. But I don't know if Uber comes way out to the sticks. And even if they do, I no longer have a phone to call them on. It goes without saying that I'm not spending the next six weeks of my life in this freak-show wellness camp. But for right now, I accept the fact that I'm stuck. The Range Rover belongs to the Oasis, not me, so there's no way back to Little Rock and the Gulfstream if Ms. Meditation doesn't approve. For all I know, the plane isn't there anymore. Vlad probably had them fly it back to California, so he can go all over the place. I can tell you where he *won't* go, that's for sure. To a wellness oasis.

First thing tomorrow, I'm out of here if I have to walk. But right now, if I don't get some food, I'm going to face-plant in the pine needles. I might as well check out these famous burgers Ivory's hyping.

She points through the double doors. "The dining hall is the larger building at the center of the cluster of cottages. Leave your bags—I'll have them brought to your cottage. Bon appétit. And be whole."

"*Hole?*" What now?

"Whole," she amends, emphasizing the *wh* sound. "As in *entire*. Your mind, body, and spirit. Be your whole self."

Like I could be anybody else. The only *hole* I want is a place to crawl into until this nightmare is over.

So Matt and I go to the dining hall. The sign over the entrance reads NOURISHMENT FOR THE BODY. There's another building close by with a NOURISHMENT FOR THE SOUL sign. That must be where Ivory and her meditation hang out. I'm definitely history before anybody makes me go there.

The dining hall is nicer than a school cafeteria, but it's basically a school cafeteria. They give you a tray; you pick out what you want; you go find a seat at one of the long communal tables. The private chefs from the good resort would probably drop dead if they had to work here.

They won't let me take two burgers. The server

15

explains—like she's talking to a five-year-old—that if I'm still hungry after I finish the first one, I can come back for seconds.

"Oh, I'll be hungry enough," I assure her. I'm so hungry I can barely focus on what a downer it is to be here.

Because it's still early, there are only a few diners scattered around the big room. I wonder how long it took them to get to the top of the waiting list. No offense, but I have zero respect for anybody who comes here on purpose instead of being tricked into it by their dad.

Matt waves me over to a spot by a big picture window. It has a view of the lake, which I can now see is a side pool of a long river.

"Pretty, isn't it?" he offers.

I don't answer. On an empty stomach, I can't muster enough sarcasm to come up with the vicious reply he deserves.

I plop myself in the chair, grab my burger with both hands, take a gigantic bite . . .

. . . and spit it out so hard that it decorates the picture window.

"That's not a burger!" I choke.

"Sure it is," Matt replies airily. "A veggie burger."

"A *what*?"

"The Oasis is one hundred percent vegetarian," he informs me like it's the most obvious thing in the world.

I reach for my pocket, determined to call Vlad and demand to be taken out of this backwoods torture chamber or else.

That's when I remember: my phone and all my electronics are locked away at the welcome center.

All this wellness is going to kill me.

More favorites by GORDON KORMAN

THE MASTERMINDS SERIES